Casualties of
Immortality

Soren Storm

Dedication

For those who love a dark tale
steeped in magic, and a trial of the human spirit.

And for Lori, for making me believe that someone from a small town
in the middle of nowhere could live their biggest dream.

Contents

Important Content Information

This story may contain sensitive material that some readers might find difficult to read. These themes include, but are not limited to violence, gore, animal death, death, murder, self-doubt leading to thoughts of endangering one's self, and explicit romantic scenes. If at any time you find yourself uncomfortable, or unable to continue reading, you are advised to put yourself first, recognize your limits, and act accordingly to protect your personal well-being.

Stolen Time

Stolen time,
To soothe the sores.
Stolen time,
To mend the flesh.
Stolen time,
To fuse the bones.
Stolen time,
To defy death's kiss.
Stolen time,
To reap the rewards.

The rewards,
Of invisible scars.
Invisible scars,
Of infinite measure.

An infinity,
Not worth living.

Not without you.

Prologue
Vigo

F rom sturdy boughs, paper lanterns cast the apple orchard in a warm glow. A crisp fall breeze swept through, carrying the scent of mead and cinnamon apple cider. The autumn harvest ended nearly a week ago, and the village was now gathered in celebration.

The sheep lazed around, happy to be used as pillows so long as there were apples to eat. And there were. Many sticky little hands fed the sheep well and full of apple slices between naps and party games.

Vigo pulled his mahogany curls into a haphazard bun. The shorter locks framing one side of his face slipped out with the evening wind. He cracked a smile at the children whizzing by in a game of tag.

He stood upon a ladder, attempting to hang another lantern, when a girl passed by with a half-eaten apple in hand. She stopped.

"Have you seen Enzo?" she mumbled with a full mouth, still chewing on an apple bite.

Vigo briefly peered over a branch and down the backside of the tree, where he noticed a little boy peeking up at him. A dark curl snagged on the tree, and he winced as he shook his head vigorously, brown eyes wide with concern.

"Are you playing hide and seek?" Vigo asked the girl as he fixed the lantern to the branch.

"Maybe," the girl half admitted.

"Then isn't asking for help cheating?"

"Yes."

"Then, no. I haven't seen him."

The little girl scoffed, crossed her arms, and wandered off with a huff.

Vigo climbed down, leaving the boy where he found him and a paper lantern hanging at a tilt. He had been running behind with his hosting duties, but the last lantern had finally been hung when a familiar figure made her way towards him. Mia's ebony twists were pushed back under a red silk bandana, and she smelled like roasted vegetables and mutton. She had been helping Vigo's brother, Jacob, cook the food. Vigo had offered to help with the vegetables, but she had insisted that she had to cook the vegetables from her farm. They wouldn't taste their best otherwise.

"Have you seen Enzo? It's nearly time to serve the guests, and I need his help just as much as Jacob needs yours."

"Game's over, kid. Time to work," Vigo called toward the tree behind him.

"Do I have to?" Enzo protested.

"Yes." Mia gave him a pointed look.

"Okay. Maya!" Enzo called. "Don't bother looking for me anymore!"

From somewhere in the distance, the small girl yelled back, "Okay!"

Tree branches shook, and leaves rustled. Enzo's grunts could be heard as he descended the tree. Suddenly, he appeared at Vigo's side, less than eager to help dish out food to a mass of hungry people.

"At least we get to eat first. It wouldn't be fair for the hosts to eat last, considering how hard we've been working," Vigo said.

"I get first plate!" Enzo shouted, and he broke into a run.

"You'll have to be faster than—"

Before he could even finish the sentence, let alone follow Enzo, Mia placed a sturdy hand on Vigo's shoulder. A sign to hang back and talk.

"Is everything okay," he asked.

Mia had a wistful smile. Her mahogany eyes shined with unshed tears. "I feel like I need to thank you."

"For what?"

"It's been hard since my husband's accident. His absence left Enzo a sullen shell of himself, but he opened back up and even plays with other kids again. And I have you to thank for that."

Vigo had noticed the change in Enzo over the last few months, but he didn't think he deserved as much credit as Mia was giving him. He stopped and took Mia's hands in his.

"Hey," he said. "You are a strong woman and an amazing mother. You and Darrian gave Enzo a strong foundation, and you continue to nurture him. Don't convince yourself that I did anything more than be his friend when other kids didn't understand how to reach out."

She nodded her head, and the two of them moved on. In the distance, the pop from a barrel of mead being cracked open echoed through the trees.

Vigo and Mia met up with Jacob at the edge of two fire pits with hot coals whose orange glow danced about in a mesmerizing pattern. One fire pit let off the scent of savory, meaty smoke. The second aired a spicy, herbal scent that melded with the smoked sheep. The sheep had been slow roasting for several hours, making the meat so tender that the dullest knife could cut through it with ease.

Mia, Enzo, Jacob, and Vigo ate together by the fire, and when they had finished, Jacob called for dinner.

Two lines formed with hungry eyes and hands full of drink. Even Jacob served patrons with one hand because his other clasped a wooden mug full of mead.

One guest after another, Vigo slapped a tender, juicy slice of mutton on their plates. He was like a machine. He said hello, he smiled, and he gave them some mutton before sending them over to Mia for their vegetables. His routine seemed to be rhythmically timed and on point. Then, an unfamiliar face stepped up in line.

Her beauty enchanted him at just a glance. Something about her pulled him from one trance and into another. Hair like streams of sunlight cascaded over her shoulders and down her gossamer dress. She had eyes like azure lakes in springtime, and a kind, carefree smile.

His nerves set something off in him. Something akin to excitement, with a twinge of fear as she approached. She looked right at him, her lips a sly smile as she said, "Your family has a knack for parties, I see."

"Supposedly the best," Vigo said.

"I certainly hope so."

She continued to smile, and he smiled back. Silence passed between them until she asked, "Can I have some?" She pointed to the smoking sheep.

"Oh!" Vigo jumped. "Of course." His face heated, and he hoped it wasn't red.

Her giggle as he placed a luscious slab of meat on her plate wasn't very reassuring. In his fluster, he offered her vegetables. She seemed delighted, but whether that was because of the attention he gave her or if it was because of how he went about it was a tossup.

Mia beat Vigo to the spoon of vegetables, though, and she gave him a look. "Don't touch my serving spoon. You still have a line waiting," she said.

"Yeah..."

Mia spooned a helping of roasted carrots and sprouts onto the young woman's plate. "Enjoy your evening," she said.

"Thank you," the young woman replied. "I'm sure I'll see you later." The mystery maiden walked off with her plate of food, leaving Vigo grappling with a tight chest and his serving duties.

After everyone had been served, he and Jacob sat in the grass near the stage. Jacob was probably on his third cup of mead while Vigo sipped cider. Enzo and Mia joined them. Mia gave Vigo an amused smile and a teasing side-eye. Vigo set his attention on how itchy the dry grass was. Mia whispered something in Enzo's ear.

"You touched Mama's serving spoon!" he blurted out.

"Yeah, what was that about? Your line deadlocked, but I was the one only using one hand," Jacob so helpfully pointed out.

"Was it that pretty lady?" Enzo asked.

Vigo felt his face heat again. The fact that he had had quite a few girlfriends and none of them had him feeling or acting this way deepened his embarrassment.

"Well," Jacob started. He stood and took Vigo by the wrist. His hands were slick with mutton juice. "If you really want to impress her, I say you get up on stage and serenade her."

Jacob tugged Vigo along by his shirt. The bartender's daughter walked by with a serving platter of drinks. Vigo snatched a glass as she passed. He instinctively took a drink as his brother hauled him onto the stage.

A lonely guitar leaned against the stage, and an elderly gentleman tuned his fiddle with a mug at his feet. A boy no older than seventeen cradled a sheepskin drum in his lap. Jacob was no singer, especially when drunk, but his feet usually kept him upright. For the most part, anyway. He stomped his feet to an even tempo and pointed at the old man and the boy who started a tentative tune. Vigo clapped his hands to the beat of Jacob's feet.

Jacob pointed at him and proclaimed loud enough for the whole party to hear. "Come on, sing for your dear brother, and get this party going!" He promptly snatched the guitar off the stage edge and pushed it to Vigo's chest.

Cheers erupted from the crowd, and Vigo happily answered their call. He strummed a jaunty tune and sang a verse of mirth. Jacob still held a mug in one hand while the other was busy flailing around with glee. They sang together and stomped around in a spin. The crowd followed suit, sending themselves into a liquor-drunk dizzy spell. Children hopped around on bare feet as the music played, and a flash of golden locks caught Vigo's eye again.

She stood on the side, clapping along. She glanced his way, and his eyes locked with hers. His heart fluttered again. He imagined that if someone were to cut his chest open, they would find his heart had grown wings, and it would soar right out of his chest. He wasn't entirely sure it wouldn't be able to fly up his throat and out his mouth as it was. He decided it was a fun feeling that he rather enjoyed.

Vigo motioned her over with a wave of his hand. Her smile was so big, the apples of her cheeks kissed the corners of her eyes. She leapt into the dancing circle and twirled. Her lacey dress billowed out. From where he stood on stage, she looked like a spring flower with her yellow hair and white dress sprawled out into petals. She danced close to the stage. So close, Vigo was sure he could reach out, and their fingertips would graze each other.

The music came to an abrupt stop. Vigo set his guitar down. Twirling kids fell into a giggling pile, and everyone's chest heaved with the rise and fall of deep breaths. Vigo scanned the crowd and nearly missed her. She was still right next to the stage, resting her head against it. Her cheeks were flushed red.

Vigo set his guitar down. Then extended a hand. She looked up at him and smiled. She seemed to do that a lot, but this smile was different. It was a mischievous side smile, and her eyes seemed to twinkle in the lantern light. She took his hand and climbed onto the stage. Her hand was soft and warm in his grasp. When their hands parted, the warmth ran away with a chill on its heels, and Vigo realized the music was back.

They stomped their feet and clapped their hands to the rhythm. The stage vibrated as if it were the heart of the party, giving life to the scene. Vigo knew the real heart was everyone there. The old man playing the fiddle sent the idle jig into a fury. The girl Vigo pulled on stage twirled so hard, she stumbled right into Vigo's chest. He held her shoulders as she laughed for so long, Vigo was surprised she hadn't passed out from the lack of air. Her hair had fallen over her face like a curtain.

Next to them, Jacob threw back whatever was in his mug and stumbled right off the stage. Children giggled, others gasped, and the music stopped. Mia and Enzo rushed to Jacob's side. After a moment, Mia called, "He's fine," and everyone went back to dancing.

The girl, in Vigo's arms, had finally calmed. She brushed her hair out of her face and looked up at him with another mischievous smile before leading him out of the crowd and towards a quieter part of the orchard.

"You know, I haven't seen you in town before. Are you a fairy intending to bewitch me? Or tricking me into the forest so you can feed me to the abandoned children the fairies keep?" Vigo jested.

"Not exactly. Besides, I believe it was you who beckoned me first."

"Noted." Vigo couldn't help but smile. This woman made him feel giddy, like a kid with a crush. "So, what's your name?" He asked this time.

She stopped walking, faced Vigo, and nearly pinned him to a tree with just her alluring gaze. "It's Sera. Also, fairies don't eat people," she said. "They definitely don't raise cannibals either."

"I had doubts about the validity of such extravagant tales, but tell me, how are you certain none of it's true, not even just a little?"

She stepped forward, and Vigo stepped back. Not in fear but want. He wanted her to follow him. To step close enough to share whispers in the autumn moonlight. It was bright and full. Maybe he would show her the stream that ran through the orchard.

"I grew up in the woods, near the fairy realm."

"How do I know you aren't lying?"

"You don't. But it's a fun story either way."

"I do love a good story." Vigo smiled like the flirt he was.

"I grew up playing with the children the fairies took in. It's true they developed magic, but nothing as fearsome and powerful as a fairy. Some of my best friends were those orphans."

"Let me get this straight. As a kid, your family let you play with witch children, but as an adult, you can't skip over to the next town for a party?"

"It's complicated."

"Sounds like it."

A silence passed between them. Not heavy—quite the opposite in fact. Vigo felt floaty, like when you drink alcohol. The calm, light feeling you get before you've drank too much and everything's funny. In the full moonlight, Sera almost glowed with a halo, or maybe it was the drink. But he was sure he only had a sip. He didn't feel like this until he'd had two mugs, at least.

"You're cute," Sera said.

Vigo laughed. "And you're beautiful."

She smiled back. Not the teasing smile, though. It was gentle, almost demure.

"I'm being honest."

"Oh, I know." This time, she smiled with tight cheeks and her tongue between her teeth. "Most people find me pleasing to the eye."

"What else do they say?" Vigo asked.

"Wouldn't you like to know?"

Vigo crossed his arms and a leg as he leaned into the tree behind him. "I would."

Sera did the one thing Vigo had been longing for; she stepped closer to him. "And what would you like to know?"

"Your hobbies. For example, do you garden?"

"You could say that."

"How so?"

"I enjoy nurturing nature." She leaned in and placed a hand on the tree behind Vigo.

"Uh-huh."

"I know you like to sing." She tilted her head.

Vigo mirrored her, and chuckled low. "I do."

"You're good at it."

"Am I?"

"You joke."

"Do I?"

"Yes." Sera's eyes dropped to Vigo's lips before meeting his gaze. "You seem to do it a lot, too."

"Life's more fun when you can joke about anything. Makes the tough stuff easier to live with."

"Is that so?"

"I think so."

"It might be fun to try that lifestyle out for a change. Mind if I stick around to find out?"

Vigo couldn't help the smile that eased its way onto his face. "How long?"

Sera stepped back, removing her hand from the tree. "I'm not sure yet. I guess I'll stay until I get bored, or my family drags me home."

"How long do you think that will be?"

"Could be hours, could be days, could be years. My family is fickle like that."

Vigo pushed off the tree and bridged the gap between them. He put a hand on either side of her arms and slid them down to hold her hands. They were soft and gentle.

"If you only had a couple hours before they came to get you, what would you do?"

Sera laughed lightly. "Aside from what I've already done this evening, there are a couple things I wanted to try."

"And what would that be?"

Sera's fingers intertwined with Vigo's. "Kiss."

"Have you never kissed anyone before?"

"No. I have. I've done a lot of things you wouldn't think I have. You asked what I wanted right now that I hadn't done yet tonight. I want to kiss you."

"Is that so?"

Sera leaned in with the hint of a smile. Vigo followed her lead, and they kissed. It was light and sweet. Her lips tasted like apple cider and honey; he hoped his tasted just as good. That's when they stopped holding hands to wrap their arms around each other. He held her snug at the waist. She placed her hands pleadingly at the back of his head. They pulled each other closer into another kiss. One deeper than before that took Vigo's breath away.

They broke apart to breathe deep. Vigo's lungs filled with her alluring scent. She smelled like the earth. Dewy moss and lilies. He realized that he probably smelled like sweat from all the dancing and singing. The thought left as soon as she kissed him again because all he could think about was her. How she smelled like a magic garden, and how she felt in his arms. Her soft body molded to him radiated a tender warmth, and her lips were so full. She was a good kisser. She did have practice. A lot of practice, if he wasn't mistaken. Luckily, he did, too.

The evening was a blur accented by moments in time that stood still only for him to bask in Sera's presence. He hoped she felt the same as they spoke of their hobbies and favorite childhood memories. She seemed to be a troublemaker. Nothing serious, though. Silly things like reading your mom's naughty books. Sera didn't specifically say that they were naughty books, but they were books she wasn't supposed to read until she was older, more experienced. To Vigo, that meant her mom's naughty books that had more sex than plot. He had read a couple of those when he was too young to do so, so he could relate. He got caught one time. Thankfully, it was by his father.

Sera stayed the night and then the next. The days turned into weeks. The weeks into months. Sera had arrived the night of the festival and simply never left.

A Love Defiant

Sera

If Sera had to pick the day she fell in love with Vigo, she would say the night they met at the harvest festival two years and six months ago.

Soft, spring sunlight enveloped the bedroom where Sera lay. Vigo's arm held her close by the waist as he dozed. His chest was warm against her back. She took his hand in hers and brought it to her lips. She kissed his knuckles. A breathy, sleepy chuckle escaped Vigo's mouth, and he nuzzled into the back of Sera's neck. His stubble grazed her skin, and she laughed.

"You're tickling me," she said between giggles.

Vigo stopped. He laid his cheek on her shoulder. "You tickled me first."

"I was giving you kisses."

"And they were lovely, dear." He kissed her shoulder.

Sera rolled over for a kiss on the lips. Vigo leaned into the kiss, and his dark waves of hair fell over the front of his shoulder. The kiss was soft and tender, and deep. Their lips parted, and Vigo appeared lost in Sera's eyes.

"It's time," Sera said.

Vigo glanced out the window. "It is," he agreed.

They pushed off the cotton covers, got out of bed, dressed, and went down for breakfast. They were drinking fresh wildflower tea with honey and eating cinnamon toast and apples when someone knocked on the door.

"I got it," Vigo said.

Vigo opened the door, and Jacob waltzed in. His tan shirt had a muddy smudge, and his hands were dusted in fine dirt. "The tree's here," he said.

"That's wonderful! Thank you!" Sera jumped out of her chair and ran to give Jacob a hug.

"Thank you," Vigo said.

A couple months prior, Sera and Vigo had gone on a trip to search for saplings and young bushes. They had found a wispy willow on a farm in Twin River. The tree wasn't yet strong enough to handle a move, but it was now, and Jacob had gone to meet the seller halfway in Lloydstone. He was back, and Sera couldn't wait to see the tree, their tree.

It was tradition for those planning marriage to pick out a tree or bush they both enjoyed and plant it together at their wedding. If a couple stayed together, when they died, they would be buried near the base. Fairies had a lot of earthly celebrations full of magic and wonder, but they didn't have birthday parties or weddings. Fairies celebrated nature, but they lived so long, they forgot to celebrate life. That's one thing Sera loved about humans; they celebrated everything they could simply because it was fun.

Sera couldn't help but smile earnestly. She wrapped her arms around Vigo and squeezed so tight he coughed.

"Sorry," she said.

Vigo's voice was deep and smooth. "Don't be."

"I'm just so excited!"

"Good..." Vigo cradled Sera's chin with his thumb and index finger. He drew her in for another kiss. It was quick and playful, and it made Sera's heart skip a beat before it burst to life again like a field of butterflies taking off. He withdrew his lips, and she bit her bottom one as she grinned.

There was another knock on the door. "Come in," Sera called.

In stepped Mia, hauling a very large burlap sack over her shoulder. "It's done just in time!"

"My dress?"

"Of course."

Sera took the bag with ease.

Enzo stepped around Mia to get to Vigo. He failed to whisper, "Dad used to look at Mom the way you look at Sera."

Vigo ruffled Enzo's hair. "Of course he did. He loved your mother."

Enzo's father was buried under a pink rhododendron bush. Mia visited him on his birthday, his death day, their wedding anniversary, at the turn of every season, and even when she just plain missed him. Enzo finally started joining her a few months back.

Thinking about Mia being widowed so young seemed to darken the room. Sera was immediately drawn to the golden bands on Mia's wrists. She had one on each. They were her and her husband's wedding rings. Sera felt the shadows in the room crowd her out. "I'm going to put this upstairs. I'll be right back down," she said.

"Do you need help, dear?"

"I'm stronger than I look. Remember?" Sera winked before she turned to head up the stairs.

She laid the sack on their unmade bed and took a seat. She tried to quiet her thoughts or at least ignore them. They told her that Mia's life now was a glimpse into her own future. Vigo was painfully mortal, and she was not. Her heart shattered like glass on a stone floor. She always knew Vigo's life was short, much shorter than hers; it just so happened to finally sink in on their wedding day of all days.

Sera wiped away the tears that threatened to spill over. She took a deep breath and smiled. Only happy tears today. Vigo was alive and healthy, and he would be for years to come. There was no sense in making herself sad on such a beautiful day.

When Sera entered the kitchen, Vigo held an arm out for a hug. She fought the urge to run to him, and when she nestled into his chest, she breathed deeply. She filled her lungs with his scent. He smelled like sun-kissed apples. "I love you," she sighed.

"I love you, too. Is everything okay?"

She let go. "Of course," she lied, and guilt squeezed her heart. She never lied, not to Vigo at least. Not since she told him she was a fairy and not just some girl who grew up living suspiciously close to the Fae Woods.

"Juniper should be here soon with the ale and wine," Jacob said.

"And Doctor Marrion and half the town should be here soon after," Vigo added. He looked down at Enzo. "Do you want to help Jacob and I set up tables and chairs, or do you want to help your mom and Sera decorate the arbor?"

"I want to help you," Enzo said.

After setting up, Jacob dragged Vigo off to get changed, and Sera followed Mia up to the bedroom to don her wedding gown.

"I love the lace..." Sera's voice trailed off. Her fingertips brushed over the lace sleeves in awe.

"I hoped you would," Mia said. She smiled so wide, her dimples showed.

Sera continued admiring the rose-patterned lace skirt. The top was a white satin corset back. Sera had sewn the dress herself with Mia's help, but Mia did the lace sleeves all on her own, Just for Sera.

"Thank you so much!" Sera hugged Mia so tightly her back popped.

"Ope," Mia said.

"Sorry!" Sera let go immediately. She looked as apologetic as she felt with her hands folded in each other.

"Don't be. I think I needed that, actually."

"I couldn't have done this without you."

"I know," Mia said proudly. "Now give it a twirl."

Sera twirled and imagined Vigo watching her with a starry gaze. Her dress flared like a blooming rose. Tears pricked her eyes, but they did not flow. They glistened with promise, waiting for the right moment to fall. Now was not that moment. Those happy tears full of love and joy she would save.

"Do you still want the two side braids to meet in the back and braided into a bun?"

"That sounds right."

Standing, Sera was a whole head taller than Mia, so Sera sat on the floor while Mia sat on the edge of the bed, braiding away. Sera stared at her simple, satin shoes in the corner. They were white, like her dress, but no one would see much of them anyway. The dress swept the floor. The train she planned to wear was also made of overlapping layers to look like a snowy waterfall of rose petals.

Mia's hands through Sera's hair paired soothingly with the warm midday sun streaming into the room. Her life in the human realm felt more like a fairytale than her life in the Fae Woods. The irony filled Sera with the fluttery feeling of laughter, and a giggle escaped her lips.

"What are you laughing about?" Mia's question was laced with cheeky amusement.

"Nothing."

Mia paused her braiding. "You're not having second thoughts, are you?"

"No, of course not. I'm just...very happy."

"Good." Mia went back to braiding.

They sat in peaceful silence the rest of the time, aside from the occasional "Hold this" or "Hand me that" from Mia.

When her hair was done, Sera slipped on her shoes, and they went down to the kitchen. Mia left Sera there, waiting for her return with the go-ahead. Sera knew the wedding location was a bit of a walk from the house and into the orchard, but the clock on the wall seemed to tick too slowly.

She recalled a jest she had made when she and Vigo met. She had told him her family would be back for her eventually, she just didn't know when. It wasn't really a joke, but as the weeks passed into a couple years, she started to believe it might have turned out to be one. As the clock ticked away above the door, she hoped it was. It would be all too cruel for this life to be ripped away from her now.

Mia finally returned, and out the door they went. They passed under the blooming branches where the orchard met the edge of the yard not even a hundred feet from the doorstep. As they ventured deeper into the orchard, the sound of water trickling over rocks and the earthy scent of damp moss filled the air. They were close.

People sat in rows turned to face her. As she walked, the orchard fell away in the presence of the sun-dappled stream, the natural break where an arching wooden bridge connected this half of the orchard and the next. An arbor covered in wildflowers and ivy lined up with the bridge. Sera's heart skipped a beat, and all the air in her lungs had been whisked away with the wind. Then she saw him standing under the arbor, and her heart fell back into rhythm, and her lungs filled with fresh air again.

She made her way down the aisle, past smiling faces, over dewy greenery that seeped into her cloth shoes, and into the arms of her lover, her fiancé, Vigo.

"You're gorgeous," he said.

"So are you," Sera replied. Her eyes swept over his dark, fitted suit. His wavy locks of mahogany hair lay over his broad shoulders. A sight that held her gaze a moment longer before her eyes met his. With a glance down the aisle, Vigo reminded Sera to watch Enzo. He came down the aisle carrying a laced pillow and a giddy grin. From atop the pillow, two golden bracelets gleamed. Their wedding bands.

Doctor Marrion cleared his throat, slicked back his hair, and began reading from a leather-backed book labeled 'Marriage Rites and Protocols.' She felt guilty for not paying attention to a single word Marrion said. All she could focus on was Vigo. His brown eyes shined like honey in the sun. His smile. Oh, his smile was a charming grin that promised a night of indulgence. She couldn't wait.

Behind him, sat upright, was their tree. It was a little thing with a thin trunk and wispy branches that grazed the ground. It was small now, but Sera knew it would grow fast. Willows love water, and it was going to root right next to this stream that trickled harmoniously.

Doctor Marrion stopped talking, letting the sounds of nature overtake the ceremony. Wind in the trees, chittering squirrels, and whistling birds were like words given to the melody of the stream. That's when he sang. Sera hadn't noticed him take up the guitar, nor had she realized that it had been propped against the arbor behind him the whole time.

Sera was in awe at the pleasant surprise. She didn't know Vigo had prepared a song for their wedding, but she should have expected it. Vigo's eyes focused on hers, and she focused on his. As the world faded away, it morphed into one all their own. To Sera, this new world was a warm, golden galaxy in the stars where animals flourished, plants blossomed, and the whole of it lived and died by Vigo's tune. He was her world, her everything. Tears pooled in the corners of her eyes as Vigo sang to her. This time, she let those tears fall. Vigo's guitar faded away before he cupped her face and rubbed his thumb across her cheekbone, wiping her tears away.

When Vigo's song ended, he kissed Sera on the forehead and hugged her close. He whispered into her ear, "I hope those are tears of joy."

Sera felt his smile against her flushing skin. "They are."

"Good. I would be heartbroken if you left me under the arbor."

"Never."

Marrion clearing his throat pulled chuckles from the audience. Sera and Vigo pulled away from each other long enough for Marrion to ask the question of the day. Their answer was a resounding, "I do."

"You may now wear your union rings."

With a cheeky smile, Enzo handed them the golden bracelets. The bands were cool to the touch, sending shivers down Sera's spine as Vigo slipped one over her knuckles and onto her wrist. She did the same for him, and finally, they kissed. It was light and fleeting, but Vigo's wink was yet another silent promise. There was more to come. The thought sent a shiver of excitement down her spine. She looked out at the cheering crowd, and that shiver turned cold. Thick clouds rolled in, blocking out the sun. A dark shroud, like a mourning veil, fell over the party. No one seemed to notice except Sera.

In the near distance, a familiar face stood amongst the apple trees. Her wings were hidden away, but Sera knew that ghostly pale complexion and sleek dark hair belonged to the foreboding figure of Elder Lobelia. If anyone noticed her, they didn't show it. Vigo placed a hand on Sera's shoulder, shifting her attention to him.

"What's wrong? Who is that?"

"You see her, too, then?"

"I can also see how you're trembling," Vigo said. He pulled her into another hug.

Vigo's warm embrace did nothing to chase away the dreadful chills Elder Lobelia gave her. "Stay here. I'll see what she wants. Distract everyone for me, will you?"

"Of course. Just be careful."

Sera walked off. Vigo kept eyes off her by suggesting a snack and drink break before the planting ceremony. Sera took a deep breath, squared her shoulders, and with every step, dug her feet into the ground. Elder Lobelia regarded her with stern displeasure.

"What are you doing here?" Sera asked.

"You broke our most important rule, never tell a mortal your name. You didn't just give him your nickname; you gave him your full name. That's just as bad as telling someone what part of the earth you were born from."

"He's harmless," Sera insisted. "And I love him, and he loves me."

"This silly wedding means nothing. It's a farce. Please tell me he doesn't know your origin."

"He doesn't," Sera lied. Of course she told him.

Elder Lobelia gave her a deadpan look and pointed towards the party. "He's going to die. I know you know that. In your lifetime, you've seen the death of an entire generation of mortals."

"I remember," Sera said. She crossed her arms and avoided looking at Elder Lobelia. "Some of them were my friends."

"That's the price we pay for taking in the children they abandon on our doorstep. Do you remember how it feels to lose them? To watch them wilt and wither like an underwatered flower?"

Sera didn't want to give Elder Lobelia the satisfaction of an answer.

"Imagine how much worse that feeling will be when it's his turn." She gestured at Vigo. "Leave him now before it's too late." Elder Lobelia went to hold Sera's hand.

Sera stepped back. "I don't want to see you again."

Elder Lobelia's face crinkled in disgust. Her voice turned sour. "He could easily betray you. Mortal men do it all the time."

"He won't," Sera insisted.

"Come home."

"I am home." Sera's heart raced as she turned away from her Elder. She expected to be dragged back by thorny vines. At the very least, shouted at. Neither happened.

Sera didn't dare look over her shoulder until she made it back to Vigo, who handed her a glass of fizzy ale. From what she could tell, Elder Lobelia was gone.

"What was that about?" Vigo asked.

"Just a concerned family member." Sera sipped her ale. The bubbly heat warmed her inside and out. Despite the dark clouds having moved on, she still saw the world as if it were obscured by shadows. "I told you they would come for me one day."

"Now they're gone again, though, right?"

"For now." Sera gulped down a mouthful of drink. She knew Elder Lobelia was the reason fairies didn't fall in love with humans. The man she fell for had betrayed her. Was it caution or jealousy that made her so persistent with Sera? She wasn't sure.

Sera downed the last bit of ale. "Let's get started."

Vigo took another sip of his drink. "Okay." Then he called Jacob over and gave him his cup of mead. "You can have this," he said.

Jacob looked at its contents, shrugged, and threw it back.

"We're starting the planting ceremony!" Vigo called.

The guests drew in close to the stream's edge. Some sat on the damp ground, nursing mugs of alcohol. Others stayed standing as they enjoyed spongey, vanilla cakes. They were called fairy sweets because of their light, airy consistency. It was a common misconception that fairies could fly, though. Their wings were almost purely decorative.

Almost. They were the key to opening the portals between the fairy realm and the human one.

Vigo grabbed the shovel that had been propped against the bridge next to the willow tree. He dug the spade into the soft earth first. *Shiiick*— was the swift and distinct sound of tiny stones scraping the shovel head. Vigo hauled out a small mound of dirt, then passed the shovel to Sera. She took the rough, grainy handle and imagined being stuck with a splinter if she wasn't careful. She shoveled out another pile of dirt and passed the shovel back to Vigo. This continued until the hole was the perfect size.

Together, they lowered the sapling into place. It fit snuggly, like a baby nestled in its mother's arms. They covered the roots, and everyone cheered. Vigo pulled Sera to his chest, planting kisses on the top of her head, but Sera was somewhere else. She was lost in a maze of her own making. Worry and heart-pounding dread came and went throughout the rest of the party. Her life didn't feel so much like a fairy tale anymore.

Until Death
Vigo

Sera and Vigo had seen the rest of the guests off at sunset. Now, they stood on the bridge over the stream, and Sera seemed apprehensive. Her intense gaze was set in furrowed brows that wrinkled her forehead as she scanned the trees.

"Who are you looking for?" Vigo asked.

Sera didn't respond. Did she not hear him? Vigo put a hand on her shoulder, and she jumped.

Vigo backed off. "What's wrong?" he asked.

Sera visibly sighed. "I'm afraid she might still be here."

"Who?"

"The woman I talked to earlier. That was one of the Elders. She didn't even send a retainer after me." Sera looked everywhere except at Vigo.

Vigo knew the Elders set the rules and even enforced them with the help of their retainers, but according to Sera, The Elders rarely did their own dirty work. This was serious.

"What exactly did she say to you?"

"She called me foolish for loving you."

Sera's eyes glossed over. She was there physically, but that was all.

"You're not foolish." Vigo wrapped his arms around her rigid form.

"She may have exaggerated, but she didn't lie outright. That's not her style."

Vigo rested his chin on Sera's head and swayed. She relaxed into him. Her hand reached up to touch his face. He leaned into her soft hand.

"Your life is a fraction of mine," Sera finally said. "When your time is up, I... I don't know what I'll do."

Vigo squeezed her tighter, like she was the one slipping through the sands of time instead of him. "I'm sorry."

"It's not your fault. It's mine." Sera swiveled in his arms. She was back and looking at him with watery eyes. "Elder Lobelia told me it would be easier to leave you now than wait."

Vigo touched his forehead to hers. "Do you believe her?"

"I can imagine walking away right now and never coming back. You would live on in my memories, and I wouldn't even have to see you die. You would eventually fade into a summer dream that brings wistful tears to my eyes, like childhood memories gone by too soon."

Vigo's heart skipped a beat. The stolen moment constricted in his chest.

"But you're not going to do that, right?"

Silence. His chest felt like collapsing under the weight of it.

"I know it wouldn't be that simple."

Vigo hugged Sera tight, and she squeezed back. For a while, they stood there on the peak of the cherry-red bridge. The sound of the trickling stream, the breeze in the trees, and Sera's soft breathing filled the air.

"Maybe I should have planned a honeymoon," Vigo said.

"We did plan a honeymoon."

Sera gave Vigo one last squeeze before letting go. She leaned over the railing. Vigo leaned into it with his back, arms crossed over his chest as he gazed down at Sera.

"That honeymoon is six months from now because you wanted me to visit the North with you," Vigo said.

"I have a friend up there I haven't seen in years. And I promise the North will enchant you."

Vigo smirked. "The way you enchanted me?"

Sera nudged Vigo's foot with hers. "I certainly hope so," she said.

Vigo laughed. It was deep and melodious. "That's something we haven't tried." He raised a suggestive eyebrow.

Sera giggled. "Well, we have six months to plan it out."

Vigo shifted from his back to his hip. He crossed one leg over the other and laid his head in his hand, elbow propped on the railing. "My dear, you could give us the freak snowstorm of the century right now, and we could try out everything that catches our fancy."

"I could," she agreed. "But I won't."

"Why not?"

Sera gave Vigo a mischievous look before trailing her gaze up and down him. A rush of tingling heat coursed from his chest to his thighs.

"I want to make you wait," Sera teased.

Vigo sucked in a breath, eyes admiring all of Sera. "What a wait it'll be."

Sera tugged on Vigo's collar, pulling him flush against her. Vigo's breath hitched in his throat. She looked up at him through her lashes, hands sliding over his shoulders and up around his neck. She planted a sensual kiss that sent tingles down his spine. Vigo let out a rich chuckle that turned breathy as Sera swayed. He wrapped Sera in a longing embrace and fell into rhythm with her. The leather cords of her corset pressed into his hands, and Vigo hummed. He struggled to resist the urge to tug on the corset bow. His fingers fiddled with the loose loops and tails.

"Go ahead," Sera said between sultry kisses.

So, he did. One steady tug and the knot unwound. Sera's dress slacked, her neckline revealing more than before. She unbuttoned Vigo's shirt with deft fingers. They slid under the fabric, caressing his chest before pushing the shirt off his shoulders and down his arms.

"You didn't make me wait very long," Vigo pointed out.

"We do this all the time. It's the romp in the snow I'm making you wait for."

Vigo made a 'hmm' noise. "I suppose so."

He kissed Sera's lips. They were soft like rose petals, and she smelled like wildflowers, earthy and aromatic. He wanted to bask in all that she was. His world was made in her image. He indulged by unweaving her corset strings one tantalizing eyelet at a time until her wedding gown fell away like a veil. In the bright, full moonlight, Sera radiated an ethereal glow.

Sera undid Vigo's pants, and he quickly abandoned them as he followed her off the bridge to the mossy stream edge. He showered her in kisses along her sides and tugged on her nipple. She giggled and moaned. He loved hearing how pleased she was. It was his pleasure to please her. The noisy stream splashed his back with cool droplets that gave him an idea.

He dipped his hands in the water flowing by and let it drip from his fingertips onto Sera's chest. She gasped, and the sound was beautiful. She shivered under his touch. He straddled her, kissing her collarbone as he rubbed his thumb back and forth across the peak of her nipple. He trailed the kisses over her breasts before taking her other nipple in his mouth. Sera arched beneath him, and her whimpering approval excited Vigo. He wanted to give her more.

Vigo kissed his way down Sera's stomach to her inner thighs. She wound her hands into his hair and lovingly scratched his scalp. He went down, stroking her clit with his tongue. A sultry gasp of pleasure escaped Sera's lips, and her wings burst to life with golden radiance. She glowed, and Vigo basked in her light. Reveling in her pleasure had him craving her satisfaction.

Vigo sucked and licked Sera's clit with passion. It was plump from his attention, filling out her clitoral hood like a blooming flower. She bucked under him, pulling his hair and a moan from his own lips. He tensed at every moan she gave him, and when she called his name, soft and pleading, he let her know how he adored her body and soul. Sera was blissfully wet when Vigo teased the rim of her core. With one last stroke of his tongue and thumb, Sera released a sound so divine, Vigo came too. In the end, they were nothing but tangled limbs and steamy breaths as they held each other close, savoring their well-spent wedding night under the silver glow of the moon. They were lulled to sleep by the whispering riverbed and the warmth of their loving embrace.

Mourning Veil
Vigo

Two weeks had passed since the wedding, and the blooms of spring apples had matured into ripe pink and gold-swirled fruit. Jacob and Vigo were picking the apples nearest the house. They were close enough for Vigo to hear Sera humming away on the porch while she spun the newly shorn wool. It was fluffy and dry from the wash. The naked sheep grazed nearby, and Millie, the black and white goat, trotted up to Sera. Millie's bell rang the whole way in a low ding, ding, ding. Sera lovingly stroked the goat's face, and she laid her head in Sera's lap.

Sera smiled at Vigo. Her tongue poked out between her toothy smile.

She's radiant, he thought.

"Are you daydreaming again, love?" she called out to him.

"Not a dream."

"Then could you be wishing that I might trade jobs with you?"

Vigo laughed. "That would be a nightmare, not a dream, and certainly not a wish. I don't have the patience for something so tedious."

Sera tilted her head towards Enzo, who was having fun climbing the apple trees. "You have more patience than you realize, but your spinning technique does appear to be lacking."

Vigo put another apple in his sack. "Exactly. So, no trading."

Sera pointed at the clothesline bowing with laundry that fluttered in the breeze. "Promise to fold the laundry tonight, then?"

"Anything for you."

Sera smirked. "Anything, except wool spinning."

"Hey!" Jacob called.

Vigo gave his brother his full attention and noticed he had already moved onto another tree.

"Why am I the only one working right now?" Jacob asked.

"I'm picking them, too," Enzo said. He pulled on an apple; it snapped from the tree, and he took a bite.

Vigo laughed as he climbed down his ladder. "You're also eating them."

Enzo shrugged his shoulders, put the apple in his mouth, and hung upside down from his knees. A little book fell from his pocket, spine up, pages open and crumpling beneath their own weight. Enzo made a noise as he took another bite of the apple.

"You're going to choke," Vigo said. He took the apple from Enzo's hand, replacing it with his book.

Vigo passed his nearly empty bag up to Jacob and took Jacob's bag full of luscious, fragrant apples in exchange. Vigo poured his weighty bag of apples into one of the collection barrels scattered around. He moved the spare ladder to the unpicked tree nearest Enzo. "What's your mom doing today?" he asked.

"Probably weeding the vegetables."

"Shouldn't you be helping her?"

"I hate weeding. So, I made a deal with her."

Vigo climbed his ladder and reached for an apple. "And what would that be?"

"I promised to finally let her teach me how to can."

Vigo went about picking apples when a spring breeze ruffled the trees. The birds chimed in with cheerful melodies.

"You let her?" Vigo asked pointedly. Out of the corner of his eye, he saw a bird swoop down to snatch a tuft of wool that had come loose from the pile on the porch.

"Well, I promised to finally pay attention and practice with some of the spring vegetables so I can help her this fall."

"Why haven't you listened before?"

Enzo swung down from the tree branch. "That used to be Dad's job. Canning. Then you started helping. I wasn't ready to take on his work. Because..."

"You don't have to say it." Vigo knew why.

Vigo hummed as he picked apples, and the birds repeated his tune. Ever since Sera suggested farming practices that were more animal-conscientious, the orchard saw more helpful wildlife. They didn't over-pick the bushes and trees, leaving more to go around for animals like birds who unintentionally sowed berry seeds. This meant less work for everyone else. Rabbits frequented the area, too, when the leftover apples fell. The poop the rabbits left behind was beneficial to the soil and nurtured the crops, so every year, there was a little more to go around for both animals and people.

Sera was akin to a fairytale princess in the way even wild animals were drawn to her. With her around, even the orchard's stream water sparkled clear like crystal and just as crisp and rejuvenating. Whenever someone would remark on how well the orchard was doing, Vigo gave Sera most of the credit because life itself seemed more fulfilling with her around. Everyone always said that was just how the world feels when you're in love.

"You're staring at her again," Enzo said.

"And why wouldn't I?"

"Because we have work to do," Jacob shouted.

Vigo turned back to gaze longingly at his love and saw her arguing with someone. She wore a gossamer gown trimmed in silver. Hair intricately braided in an updo. Sera had her arms crossed and stepped back from the stranger. Vigo regarded her as a stranger, but somehow, she was familiar. He climbed down the tree to make his way over.

He put himself between them and offered Sera a comforting hand to hold behind his back. She took it and squeezed.

"What's going on?" he asked.

The stranger regarded him with an air of disdain. As if she saw him as lesser than. "I came to see what my daughter has been up to for the past two years."

So that's what this is, he thought. An overbearing mother tracked down her daughter. The problem with that was Vigo knew fairies didn't have children, at least not with each other. All fairies were born from the earth. Vigo remembered that Sera once told him she was born from a lily flower wilting at sunrise. Sera never talked about the other fairies, and Vigo didn't pry. He always assumed they were unpleasant. Now, he was sure of it.

"She's been with me," Vigo said.

"Yes, I can see that. I'm sure she's had fun here, too. But she needs to come home."

"She's a grown woman, and she doesn't have to do anything she doesn't want to."

Sera's 'mother' appeared to look right through him. "You've had your fun for two years without heed of consequence, and now you can't even defy me to my face? We have rules for a reason."

Sera was silent.

"Does he even realize—"

"Leave him out of it!"

Vigo was stunned. He had never heard Sera yell before. She even pushed him aside to scowl at her 'mother.'

Sera's 'mother' gestured to all of Vigo. "You're being foolish. Look at him."

Sera did. "I'm not hurting anyone by loving him."

"No one but yourself, eventually. Tell me, is he really worth it? Are you prepared to love him until the end?"

Sera was silent, her face stern.

"Are you prepared for what that will do to you?"

"Yes," Sera said.

"All right. Let's test it, shall we?"

Sera's 'mother' grabbed Vigo by his shirt collar, pulling him into her arms where she held him close. The embrace was anything but tender. He could feel her sneer before she kissed him behind the ear.

"Hey!" Sera shouted. She pulled Vigo back into her chest.

The whole interaction gave Vigo whiplash. He suddenly felt weak. His body was too heavy to support itself. His head was fuzzy, and his heart beat out of his chest. He went slack into Sera's arms. "I don't feel well," he muttered.

"You're a cute kid," Sera's 'mother' said. "And you seem really sweet. But some lessons have to be learned the hard way, and it's better to learn them sooner rather than later." She was so matter-of-fact.

"Get out of here!" Sera screamed at the top of her lungs. Her pitch reached heights that left Vigo's ears ringing and throbbing in pain.

Through blurry eyes, he watched Sera's 'mother' leave. Her face was devoid of emotion. Sera settled in the grass and laid Vigo's head in her lap. She frantically brushed his hair away from his left ear.

"What's going on?" Jacob asked.

Vigo couldn't see anyone clearly, and fear squirmed its way down Vigo's chest and into his stomach. He heard the tears in Sera's voice as she called for Enzo. He rushed over. Her voice was unsteady as she said, "You need to go home now."

"What's wrong with him?" Enzo asked.

"Nothing I want you to worry about. Now go home. Please."

"I can get the doctor."

"A doctor won't fix this. Please, go home."

He rushed off like Sera asked.

Jacob crouched down. "What's happening to him?"

Vigo wondered the same as panic spurred his heart to gallop out of his chest. His body ached, and something in him knew he was dying.

Sera held Vigo's head in the crook of her arm. Her tears splashed on his cheek.

"I'm so sorry," she sobbed into his hair.

Vigo felt a deathly chill frost over his bones like a suffocating shroud. He reached out to her with a comforting touch, but his hands and fingers were so numb he couldn't even bend his pinky. He didn't understand why it was happening. He only knew that he was dying, and he wasn't ready. He didn't want to leave Sera behind. He didn't want to leave Jacob, or Enzo, or Mia. He wanted to keep living. His body wouldn't move, and his vision was poor, but he was determined to hang on as long as he could.

Sera lifted her head, but Vigo couldn't make out her face. His vision was dark and blurred. "Dying wouldn't be so bad if I could see your beautiful face," he said.

She laughed bitterly. "Will you let me save you?"

"How—" Vigo heaved with coughs. His lungs were desperate for air as his breathing grew shallow.

Sera patted Vigo's chest and hushed him. "I can use magic," she said. "I won't lie, though. This magic is rarely used. I don't know if it will even work, but—"

"Do it."

"Hold on a minute!" Jacob shouted. "No one has explained anything to me, and suddenly, magic can solve the problem? What about a doctor?"

Sera laid Vigo in the grass. The blades tickled the back of his neck.

"Can you people not hear me? What the hell is going on?!"

"Jacob, get me wood and a bucket of water!" Sera shouted back. Vigo didn't miss the fear in her voice as her pitch suddenly climbed again.

Jacob scoffed and groaned, but he listened.

Sera searched Vigo's pockets with frantic hands.

"What—are you—looking for?" Vigo choked out.

Her hands patted over his pockets again. "Your knife."

"Back pocket." Every muscle in Vigo's body felt like it was being torn apart as he tried to roll over. Sera reached into his back pocket and pulled out his knife before rolling him onto his back again.

Sticks clattered to the ground next to him with muffled, hollow clunks. Sera moved quickly. The sound of scraping dirt gave Vigo a foreboding chill that made his hair stand on end. There was another clatter of sticks.

"Give me your flask," Sera said.

"He needs a doctor, not a drink and a soothing rest by the fire," Jacob argued.

"A doctor isn't going to do anything! We'd be lucky if a doctor even made it in time!"

"And how is drawing pictures in the sand supposed to help?"

Sera let out a primal growl of frustration. Vigo pictured the tears in her eyes as she pleaded, "Just trust me, dammit!"

"Do it," Vigo mustered. His plea was terse, and his voice small and airy. He was running out of time.

"Fine," Jacob said.

Vigo painfully gasped for air as his lungs seemed to fold in on themselves. He cried out but barely made a sound. Tears rolled down his cheeks as his body screamed for release.

The sound of splashing water drowned out the birds and branches shaking in the breeze. Something heavy hit the dirt, sending up dust.

A flash of orange light and a wave of heat whooshed to life. The smell of burnt wood permeated the air.

"What the hell was that?" Jacob shouted.

He didn't get a response. Jacob whipped around to give Vigo a look, a look Vigo couldn't see clearly. Sera unscrewed the flask and poured it out. Dancing flames reflected off the mead cascading into the fire. Sera clicked the knife open. The silver blade glinted. With her back turned to Vigo, she sucked in a breath.

The horrified look on Jacob's face told Vigo he had figured it out.

"Regular magic is one thing, but blood magic is a whole 'nother story!"

"Do you want him to die?" Sera sounded exasperated.

Vigo's throat convulsed. His blood pumped in his ears to a deafening roar as his heart smashed against his rib cage, longing for air.

The earthy smell of lilies and dewy moss enveloped him in a warm embrace. Sera held him to her chest, rocking him as she placed wet kisses on his forehead. Sera's steady stream of tears splashed on his cheeks. They were warm, and they shined like shooting stars as they passed by his dimming gaze.

Sera lifted Vigo like he weighed nothing. It barely registered as she carried him inside the house, up the stairs, and laid him on the bed. He was numb...and then nothing at all.

From Humble Pleas...

Sera

Sera pulled Vigo into her lap. His head rolled to one side. His mahogany waves draped over her thigh. He was still. Deathly still. Sera felt the vein in his neck with her fingertips. He was cool to the touch. It gave Sera shivers that chilled her own skin and pricked all the hairs on her body. She waited for a heartbeat as she watched his chest. His heart never thumped, but his chest rose ever so slightly. It was so faint; she could have imagined it.

Her heart was beating fast enough for the both of them, so She took a deep breath before brushing Vigo's hair away from the nape of his neck. Behind Vigo's ear was a spiraled brand. Elder Lobelia had given Vigo, The Kiss of Death. A curse of mortality. Sera hoped she had saved Vigo from the fate of an early death, but the mark was still there. Angry tears filled her eyes and spilled over hot and heavy. They raced down her face, dripping onto the apple of Vigo's cheek. A small muscle in his cheek twitched, and the pool of tears continued down his face.

"Love?" Sera wept. Her voice trembled.

There was no response.

Sera took Vigo's hand in hers and squeezed. His pinky twitched.

"Vigo, please, wake up," she pleaded between sobs. There wasn't enough air in the room. It was hard to breathe through her nose. Mucus had stopped it up. She sniffled to little effect.

"No! Please!" she shouted, not at Vigo but at the world itself.

She stayed with him for several hours, rigor mortis never set in. Every sign pointed to him being dead, but he wasn't. He was trapped between the two opposites of existence. Her heart ached at the thought, but she was going to fix it. She was going to fix everything. Sera planted a kiss on Vigo's forehead before getting up.

She yanked open the bedside table drawer, and its contents rattled: Loose paper, a leather-bound book, a frayed quill, some twine, and the Wander Stone. She swiped it, shoved it into her pocket, and headed downstairs.

In the kitchen, Jacob leaned back in his chair, whittling a chunk of wood. Curly shavings littered the floor and stuck to his shirt.

"I'm going out," Sera said.

Jacob sat up, smacking the chair onto all fours again. "Is he awake?"

"No." Sera wiped her face.

"I don't understand."

Sera opened the coat closet and donned one of the dark cloaks. "I have to get help." She wasn't going to ask for help; she was going to demand it.

"I thought the doctor couldn't fix this."

"He can't." Sera shut the coat closet with more force than needed or intended. "I'll be back. Watch over him, please."

"Of course I will, but—"

Bang!

Sera shut the front door and stepped out into the brisk night air. From her pocket, she withdrew the Wander Stone. It was cool and smooth in her hand. She warmed it with the heat of her palm as she concentrated on the swirling, compass-like sigil etched on its surface. She whispered where she wanted to go. The wind whipped around her, and her entire being was tugged Southward.

In the blink of an eye, Sera's surroundings changed. No longer was she standing in her front yard with a view of the orchard. She stood in the middle of a quiet town where no dogs barked and no lights lit up windows. The silence was an eerie one, as if the town was hiding from something.

Sera approached the wilderness at the edge of town. It was a great forest, thick with ancient trees and lush undergrowth. That is what the town was hiding from, the gaze of the Southern Fae Forest.

The path she followed through the thicket was narrow and winding. It converged with many animal trails, all of them slender and lined by tall grass. A cool breeze blew by, rustling the greenery into twisted spires. Sera didn't bother pulling her cloak tight or pulling over her hood. The chill in the air was welcome. Her skin flashed hot as her blood boiled with furious determination. Sera had her mind made up. She was going to demand help from the Southern Fae Council. If anyone would help her save Vigo, it would be them. She hoped she could appeal to them by claiming the Western Fae Council had passed a harsh and unfair judgment. After that, she wished to never see or hear from any Fae Council again.

Sera stormed down her path, and like lightning striking a tree, she found her mark in the place all the Southern Fae Forest roads end: The Moon Gate. There were only two. One was here, and the other in the Western Fae Wood. The doorway between worlds stood before her. Moss-covered stones wedged together in a bewildering, circular archway. The magic in the air was like static pricking her skin. She took a deep breath, letting the spell of concealment fall away. Like a butterfly, her glittering golden wings emerged. They emanated a soft glow that chased away the shadows of the night.

She remembered the way Vigo's jaw dropped in awe at the sight of them. She missed him—his deep, melodious voice, his soft and warm embrace, his mere presence full of charm. Sera worried for him, too. Her heart trembled at the thought that she hadn't saved him, and maybe the Elders wouldn't, or even couldn't save him.

She shuddered and shed those thoughts like old skin, restricting, irritating, and an overall hindrance. She walked on the mossy stone path that led right up to the Moon Gate. The gate hummed faintly. Sera reached out. Her fingertips passed through the portal, sending ripples across its translucent surface that wavered between two images. The first, the dense, dark forest. The second, a whimsical and colorful passage of blooming fronds. Shoulders square, Sera ventured into the portal and down the lush tunnel.

The brush tunnel gave way to a field of sun-dappled, knee-high wildflowers. Swinging bridges connected the redwood forest treetops to an ancient redwood tree rooted in the center of it all. That's where Sera was headed. The Elder Tree was a living tower, a castle with not only the oldest library in existence but the Southern Throne Room, too. The room Sera was going to get answers and assistance.

The Elder Tree's vast root system twisted its way into nearly every corner of the Southern Fae Forest. It was the mother tree, and like a good mother, she was connected to all living plant life, from the smallest patch of moss upon a toadstool hat to the tallest leaf brushing against the clouds. Her roots made the ground an uneven trek. Other fairies passing by paid her no mind. Sera wasn't an unfamiliar face—at least she didn't used to be. She just hoped she hadn't missed calling hour and that she still had a 'friend' on The Council.

Bloody Beginings
Vigo

Vigo awoke to a burning sensation on his cheek. Rays of morning sun filtered into the bedroom through sheer, white curtains. He recoiled at the pain that formed into tender blisters. He rolled off the bed and cowered in its shadow. His head pounded, and his throat was dry and scratchy like he had swallowed dirt.

"Sera!" Vigo struggled to call out. His throat ached too much.

He pulled the blanket off the bed and wrapped it around him before heading for the door. Everything seemed too bright as he descended the stairs. A wave of dizziness washed over him, and he leaned against the stairwell for support. His chest heaved heavy breaths as he steadied himself.

He peered around the kitchen with bleary eyes. It was empty and quiet. That's when Vigo heard a faint, *thwack, thwack, thwack from outside.*

Is she chopping wood? He thought to himself. Vigo walked through the kitchen with his back turned to the window. He stopped at the front door and leaned against it for support. His body was weak. His limbs were heavy and slack. His fingers ached with a strange tingle as they clutched the blanket wrapped around him. He doubted he had the strength to even open the door, so he yelled.

"Sera!"

No answer.

"Sera!" He feebly pounded against the door.

"Sera!" He yelled again.

The doorknob turned. The latch clicked, and the door flew open so suddenly that Vigo fell forward.

"Vigo!" said a familiar voice, edged in concern.

Dirt-smudged hands smelling of lichen helped him stand. It was Jacob. His brow, and white shirt were damp with sweat.

"Where's Sera?" Vigo asked. He leaned into Jacob's chest. The sweat-soaked shirt was cool against his cheek.

"She went out, but she'll be back," Jacob assured him. He shuffled Vigo back into the house and into a chair.

"Where did she go?" Vigo laid his throbbing head on the table and hid from the sun.

"She didn't say." Jacob peeked under the blanket at Vigo.

Vigo snatched it shut. "Can you please put up the black curtains?"

"Sure," Jacob said.

Vigo could hear Jacob moving around the kitchen. Cabinets opened and shut. Metal rings jingled. A flame crackled to life near Vigo on the table.

"You can stop hiding now," Jacob said.

Vigo pulled the blanket down and relaxed in the dark room. A candle flickered on the table, casting a small wooden figure devoid of any real shape in a serious light.

Jacob gave Vigo a discerning once over. "Your eyes, they look bloodshot. No, that's not right. Your irises are just red. What happened to you?"

Vigo wondered the same thing. He felt awful. Could he be ill? Ill was better than dead, he supposed. But what he had experienced didn't feel like something you come back from.

"I'm still not feeling well, I guess," Vigo said.

"And what's with the rash on your face?"

Vigo faintly remembered the searing pain on his cheek that woke him up. He touched his face with tentative hands. His fingertips grazed a patch of tender, warm bumps that oozed.

"Sunburn. I think."

"Should I get the doctor?"

Vigo waved the idea off. What he really needed was a drink. He pointed at the ceramic jug on the counter. "I need water."

"Oh. Sure."

Jacob got Vigo a glass and sat again. Vigo gulped the water down. It tasted like ash, making him thirstier.

"You should probably eat something, too," Jacob said. He plucked an apple from the fruit bowl on the table and rolled it toward Vigo. It deftly thumped its way across the table, where Vigo caught it in his open palm. It was then he realized the hunger pains twisting his stomach. He could smell that familiar, sweet apple scent even before lifting it to his mouth. He bit into the apple with a satisfying crunch, but his teeth suddenly felt strange. His bite was awkward.

He anticipated the tart overtones and sweet undertones of the juicy fruit, but that's not what he tasted. The flavor lacked its classic sensations. It was more akin to water—ashy water.. He must have made a face because Jacob made a comment.

"Is it not ripe?"

"It smells ripe," Vigo said. "I think I might be sick. It doesn't taste very good."

"Let me try it."

Vigo handed Jacob the apple. He flipped it to the opposite side and took a bite.

"Tastes fine to me," he said. He dug his pocketknife out of his pants to cut off the area Vigo ate from. He stopped before he even started slicing. "You got a weird bite pattern, buddy."

"What do you mean?"

Jacob held the apple close to the candlelight, then continued cutting away the side of the apple Vigo had contaminated.

Vigo only saw a glimpse, but it was odd-looking. He moved his tongue around his mouth, feeling his teeth. He ran his tongue over his canines and winced. Blood mixed with saliva as he swallowed, leaving a coppery taste in his mouth. He didn't remember his teeth being so sharp...or long.

Vigo suddenly became aware of his heartbeat and how loudly Jacob chewed. "Maybe you should try some cheese," Jacob suggested.

He did. It was worse than the apple. It wasn't smooth and savory. It was bland, bitter, ashy again, and it made his stomach upset.

"I can't eat anymore."

"That taste bad, too?"

"Worse. I might have stomach flu."

"Should I make soup?"

Despite not feeling himself, the hunger pains were hard to ignore. "I think that might help."

"Then I'll get right on it." When Jacob got up from the table, the chair squealed against the floor. He tossed the apple core in the compost bucket and started routing through the cabinets.

Vigo laid his head back on the table. Everything was too much to process. The smell of garlic in the air as Jacob peeled the flakey outside. The *thunk* of the knife hitting the cutting board after each and every crisp slice through a juicy onion. The blood that pumped in his ears.

Then the water boiled. It was a deep bubbling, so full and resonant, Vigo felt it vibrate in his chest.

"So, how long have you known?"

"Known what?" Vigo groaned.

"About Sera. She's not human, right?"

"No. She isn't."

Jacob stopped chopping.

"She told me when I proposed a year ago. She said that if we were serious, I should know. That's when she told me she was a fairy."

Jacob started chopping again. His rhythm was faster. More erratic.

"Do you tru—Damn!" Jacob yelled.

Vigo's head shot up. "What happened?" he asked. Something metallic scented overpowered the garlic and the onion.

"I cut myself."

Jacob held a rag over his hand. "It's not deep. It should stop soon."

Vigo stared at Jacob's hand wrapped in the thin, white cloth. A tiny patch of red bloomed, and just like the copper smell in the air had masked all others, the sound of a heartbeat drowned out all other sounds, even that of the roiling boil.

He noticed a prominent vein in Jacob's neck. He swore he could see it pulsing gently and bobbing as he sucked in a breath. Vigo's heartbeat was louder now, but when he placed a hand over his chest, there was nothing. He couldn't feel his heart thump once.

"That sucks. I cut it on a crease," Jacob said. "Are you all right?"

Jacob's words were lost to the humming of a heartbeat in Vigo's ears. It was an alarming sensation to hear your heartbeat and not feel it in your chest. It morphed into an enchanting hum that called him toward something. Toward someone. Vigo's gaze once again landed on Jacob, and a bell rang. Suddenly, his mind and body were not his own as he stood up with wanton vigor and sent his chair clattering onto its side. Vigo closed the gap between him and his brother in a stride. He grabbed Jacob's wrist tight, and Jacob yanked it back. He rubbed the red mark Vigo left.

"You're strong for someone who looks like death warmed over."

That steady song of heartbeats was broken by nervous flutters and the whoosh of blood. Vigo came to for a moment. "Something is terribly wrong," he said, and he was gone again.

Everything else was a blur of wailing cries and a warm, crimson river. Vigo indulged himself in Jacob's blood. It was warm and savory. So full of flavor compared to everything else he had consumed that day. Both hunger and thirst were finally satiated.

When his vision cleared again, he laid eyes on the carnage he had caused. He was petrified, stone still. Bloody saliva dripped from his lips and onto his knees like the soft, pitter-patter of rain against a tent. He bent over and heaved dry coughs, but nothing came up. The blood in the air was such a nice smell, and when he fully realized what the thought meant, he wretched again. A mouthful of blood and spit splattered onto the floor. Several droplets hit the back of his hand, and he wiped it off on his clothes. Overwhelming fear washed over him like a tidal wave and knocked him back into a chair leg.

"What am I?" He whispered to himself. He killed Jacob. There was no denying it. The room was quiet with stunned silence. He no longer heard that sound. The heartbeat song came and went with Jacob. It was his heartbeat Vigo heard. It was Jacob's life force singing, calling out, and Vigo had answered it. A mournful quiet fell over the room like a heavy blanket in summer, stifling.

Looming Dark
Vigo

V igo kept watch in the dark. His gaze was transfixed on Jacob's lifeless body. Every flicker of candlelight sharpened his facial features. It was like a beacon, calling Vigo to look at what he had done. The blood on the floor had begun soaking into the wood. It turned from a glossy, crimson puddle into a burgundy, matte stain. Vigo knew in his gut that he would never forget what happened. He told himself he wouldn't let that happen because he deserved to carry the full weight of the crushing guilt every hour of every day. Now, his floorboards would be a visual reminder to keep him accountable for that promise.

Any sound that even remotely resembled footsteps or talking had Vigo waiting by the door, ready to collapse into Sera's arms and beg her to assure him he was all right. That she still loved him because he didn't think he could love himself ever again. He needed someone else to do that for him. To forgive him.

He lost himself in the woodwork of the kitchen. Every tree line and dark spot had been poured over at least once. He counted them all because he saw them all, even in the dim lighting.

He had been counting them a second time when there was a knock at the door. Vigo tip-toed around Jacob, and guilt hooked his heart and wrenched it down. He opened the door just enough to poke his head out.

"Vigo..."

Enzo and his mother blocked the golden, peachy rays of sun. It haloed them, and Vigo feared them stepping aside.

"You don't look well," Enzo said.

"I don't feel well," Vigo agreed.

Mia gave an apologetic smile. "I'm sorry for bugging you. Enzo told me about what happened yesterday. We're worried."

The gesture made Vigo feel that much guiltier. He didn't deserve the kindness of his neighbors. He didn't deserve their friendship or their worry. "Thank you. It means a lot."

"I can get the doctor for you?" Enzo suggested.

"Don't. I'll be fine."

Mia attempted to peer inside. Vigo adjusted to block as much of the view as possible. "Is Sera here?" she asked.

"No."

"Where is she?"

"I don't know."

"I'm sure she will be back soon," Mia said.

"Me too." Vigo hoped she would, but part of him felt unsteady at the thought of her coming home to find him like this.

"Do you mind if I play in the orchard?" Enzo asked.

Vigo wanted to tell him no. That he should stay as far away from the farm as possible. "Yes, but I have a new rule for you. Do you think you can promise me to follow it?"

"Of course!"

"You have to leave an hour before sunset." Vigo figured Enzo would be safe enough during the day. Vigo didn't think he could outlast the sunlight, so if Enzo was safe at home way before dusk, he would be fine.

"I promise." Enzo offered his hand for Vigo to shake.

Vigo couldn't bring himself to do it. He mustered a smile instead. "Good," he said.

"Get well soon," Mia said.

Vigo shut the door. After it clicked tight, he let out a breath and leaned against the door. How long had he been holding his breath? He wasn't sure. He didn't feel starved for air.

Jacob's pale corpse startled him when he looked down at the floor. The renewed shock was like a knife in the heart. It stole his breath and his strength. He had to sit. He slid down the door and hugged his knees.

Night crept in at an agonizing pace. Still no Sera. Vigo couldn't leave his brother on the kitchen floor to rot. He deserved a funeral, but digging a grave took time. It would take all night just to do that, and by the next evening, Jacob would start to smell. Flies had already snuck their way into the house. They buzzed an insanity-inducing tune. Vigo couldn't take it. He was already damned, but he would be more so if he let insects and vermin use his brother as their nest.

He forced himself to stand. Despite the ache in his stiff muscles, moving was nice. He went outside and found the dead apple tree Jacob had been chopping the other day. The stump clung to the earth with weak roots. Vigo carried the logs by threes to the fire pit. They were surprisingly light. He laid them in rows, covering the ground inside the brick-lined ring.

Vigo went back inside for Jacob. He picked him up by his armpits. Jacob was stiff, and Vigo knew the chill he emanated would haunt him until the day he died. Vigo felt like he was trapped in a nightmare. Part of him couldn't believe what he had done, or why, or the fact that Sera still hadn't returned. He told himself to wait. *Do what you have to do. Get Jacob into that pit and let him go. Sera will be back.*

He needed her to come back.

Vigo walked through the middle of the pit as he dragged Jacob into place. He circled Jacob with apples. Then he went back inside one last time for matches and a drink, and he swiped the wooden figure off the table, stuffing it in his pocket.

"I'm sorry, brother," he said.

He took a ceremonial and impulsive drink from his bottle of mead. It was absolutely flavorless, aside from being uncharacteristically bitter for mead, and the ash of course. As he choked it down, he tried to remember how fine the drink used to taste. He did it to pretend some kind of normalcy—for his sake and his brother's, he supposed.

Vigo stepped into the pit with his brother. The old ash stirred up into a dust cloud, coating his brown leather shoes and turning them gray. He lifted Jacob's head and raised the bottle of mead to his lips. Mead was his favorite; Vigo figured the least he could do for his brother was send him on his way with a sip. *He might have liked a party better,* Vigo thought. He poured the rest of the bottle out on the wooden bed Jacob slept on. That's what Vigo told himself. Like a child, he would rather pretend that Jacob was trapped in a nightmare with him and the only way to set him free was with fire. It was poetic if not a blatant lie.

He sat the bottle between Jacob's arm and his side before stepping back out of the fire pit. Vigo laid two branches of brush on Jacob, like a burial veil. Vigo imagined it more like a blanket. He lit a stack of matches and tossed them onto the pyre. The brush caught fire with a bright, crackling flash. He watched the apple stems catch fire.

Flames licked their peels until they charred black. The apples hissed and popped as they boiled from the inside out.

The brush collapsed, sending hot ash flying. Jacob's alcohol-drenched clothes caught fire. Orange coals crackled and sparked. Vigo was mesmerized by their dancing glow. Tears welled in his eyes, and his vision fractured like light through fine-cut crystal.

...To Lofty Demands

Sera

T he Elder Tree was a tower of stairs and rooms. At a glance, any outside human would assume it was dead due to the hollow center. They would be wrong. Sera admired the Elder Tree's wave-patterned wood grain. When her fingertips skimmed the polished walls, a serene power washed over her and, with it, a sense of belonging. It was strange to belong to a place she no longer considered home. She had been away from the Fae Realm for a short time, but it already felt like a lifetime ago. She had changed so much in just two years, and yet she imagined Vigo would say that she was the same enchanting soul he met on the night of the harvest festival.

She made her way up to the first landing of many. Voices too muffled for Sera to hear clearly hummed against the wood door. She turned the knob of twisted roots, and it opened for her. The calling room had a curved shape, like the section of a wide and winding hallway. Two people milled about the empty space. One was a young man, human, wringing his hands and fretting over something Sera didn't care enough about to remember. The other, a fairy. The door attendant.

Sera demanded an audience with the Southern Fae Council. He insisted she wait her turn. When she opened her mouth to protest, he simply sighed, rolled his eyes, and declined to hear her out. So, she waited. She waited for the fretting man to have his meeting. Apparently, he was a librarian.

Every moment that ticked by was like a freshly sharpened knife shortening her nerves cut by cut, filleting her patience to nothing. She needed to save Vigo, and soon. Unfortunately, formality was anything but fast. Even more unfortunate was the fact that she had to at least appear composed if she was going to get any help for her very messy predicament. Worst-case scenario, her request is refused outright, and Sera is once again left to her own devices. Best case scenario, the Southern Fae Council offers aid despite the Western Fae Council's protests, potentially pitting the two sides against each other. Two sides that are supposed to work together to oversee the Fae Realm.

By the time the nervous librarian had emerged from the throne room, Sera had wrung her skirt into a heap of bunchy wrinkles, but she was finally going to get her audience. Sera had barely taken two steps into the throne room when the pair of double doors she entered through closed behind her. They sealed shut with overgrown roots. Their echoing, creaking groan as they locked into place was a foreboding contrast to the bright fairy lights dancing about.

In the center of the room, five thrones gilded in gold and plush with moss sprouted from the polished redwood floor. Each chair was filled with an Elder donned in flower crowns and gossamer gowns beaded with fine stones. A retainer stood behind each of them. The next council members in training. It was then Sera realized how little power she had. Her fate, and more importantly, Vigo's fate, was in their hands. She only hoped the Elders were feeling benevolent.

Elder Sorrel, a redhead with a surly countenance, leaned forward in his chair. "What are your inquiries, Lily Fairy Seraphine?"

Sera straightened her shoulders and smiled kindly. She recalled Elder Lobelia and the rest of the Western Fae Council keeping her relationship a local issue. She had to broach the topic delicately. "Are you aware of my disagreement with the Western Fae Council?"

"We are not," he said.

"What appears to be the problem?" Elder Dahlia asked. She wore braids adorned with golden bands. Her compassionate smile nearly let her freckled dimples show.

Sera had to contain the hope Elder Dahlia's soft looks gave her. Maybe she had an ally on The Council. They had been friends once. Dahlia used to be like a much older sister to Sera. Time simply got in the way of it all.

"A member of the Western Fae Council has wronged someone important to me."

"Go on." Elder Sorrel seemed unimpressed.

Aside from Dahlia, the other members of The Council were harder to gauge.

Sera struggled to decide on how much to tell them. She had spent an hour waiting for this meeting and wasted it with worry instead of planning the perfect approach. She couldn't incriminate herself until after they saved Vigo's life.

"Elder Lobelia used The Kiss of Death curse on a good friend of mine."

The room thickened with tension. Now, Sera was sure she had even Elder Sorrel's rapt attention. Dahlia's smile fell. Her eyebrows set in concerned concentration.

"Is it the right to revenge you want?" Another Elder asked.

"No," Sera said. "I simply want the curse reversed."

Dahlia's doe eyes shined in the fairy light. "Dear... That's not possible."

Bullshit! Sera thought. They just never tried hard enough. There had to be a way to bring Vigo back. She had to convince them to try.

"How many times have you attempted to bring someone back?"

Silence.

Dahlia looked at her like she was a newly formed fairy. The memory of Dahlia consoling a young Sera after the loss of her pet rabbit haunted her like a ghost in the back of her mind. He had died of old age and a failing body. Nothing else. That was Sera's first taste of tears from a mortal's death.

"How many?" Sera repeated. Her voice was stern, but her watery eyes betrayed her.

Elder Sorrel scoffed. "It simply isn't done. Bringing someone back from the dead is wholly unnatural and ill-advised."

Sera took a deep breath to cool the burning frustration heating her cheeks. She was going to have to admit that she had tried and failed to counter The Kiss of Death. "He's not really dead yet," she admitted.

Whispers broke out between the Elders and their retainers. Dahlia had her retainer taking notes.

"Can you elaborate for me?" Dahlia asked. Her retainer paused his note taking.

Sera blinked away her tears with magic. It was a little spell to help her save what respect The Council still had for her. If any. "I performed an experimental spell of sorts to counteract The Kiss of Death before it had finished the job. Unfortunately, my—my friend remains unconscious but alive."

"Let's take a moment to reflect before we get carried away here," another Elder spoke up. Until now, she had been relatively silent and steely-eyed. "For now, never mind your lofty request of raising the dead and the even more unbelievable claim to have halted The Kiss of Death and instead redirect our attention to why this is happening at all?"

She paused, and Sera bit her tongue to stop herself from saying something she would regret. She had so many sharp, hot, unkind words burning their way down her throat. Only some of them were for Dahlia, who had yet to stand with her.

"Now I beg the question," the Elder continued. "What did your friend do to draw such ire that an Elder of The Western Council saw fit to ensure his death with a curse?"

Sera bit her lip. She had to incriminate herself. "He didn't do anything. I fell in love with him."

There was that look again on Dahlia's face. The one brimming with pity.

"And what did you do in response to this love?" The Elder eyed the golden bracelet on Sera's wrist with scrutiny. She knew.

Sera was sure the question was meant to make her feel ashamed. She wasn't. She held her hand up for everyone to see. "I married him."

"There it is. You broke a law, and The Western Fae Council delivered the punishment they deemed just."

Sera balled her fists so tight her knuckles turned white. "Justice? It was jealousy! Elder Lobelia personally carried out my 'punishment.' We all know she's why the rule exists. Her bad decisions shouldn't dictate what I get to do with my life!"

"You forget yourself, Lily Fairy Seraphine!" Elder Sorrel's voice echoed off the wooden surface of the room.

"Elder Sorrel, calm down." Dahlia finally spoke up. "The punishment was crueler than necessary."

"Of course, you would think that," Elder Sorrel said.

"Dismissing each other and our kin's concerns is unbecoming and a bad example for our retainers."

Another Council member cleared his throat. "I agree. I think we should take the time to discuss all the information that has been given to us in private. We can reconvene at a later hour."

A later hour? That was time Sera wasn't certain Vigo had. "Please listen when I tell you—"

"You listen." Elder Sorrel dominated the room again. "You are lucky we didn't send you away from the start. Now leave us."

A sense of complete failure sunk in as Sera was escorted from the throne room. It was tempting to slip away while they bickered for hours. She could check in with Jacob and see Vigo. It would have made her feel better, at least. She didn't leave. She couldn't because if she left, there was no guarantee that The Council wouldn't dismiss her case on the grounds of absence. Waiting for old people to decide the fate of the youth quickly became Sera's least favorite past-time.

Several hours had passed since Sera's audience with The Council. The doors separating the calling room and the throne room creaked open. Dahlia stepped in and sent the door attendant away. Sera eyed her with knitted brows.

"What's happening?"

Nothing.

Something felt off. Dahlia stood with her hands clasped together over her waist as the door attendant hurried out of the room. Dread quickened her pulse and turned her stomach. The sound of the door slamming behind the fleeing attendant was reminiscent of a hammer pounding the last nail in a coffin. In this case, Sera imagined it was Vigo's coffin.

The Council wasn't going to help her. She knew it before Dahlia rushed over to her with that pitiful look in her eyes. She felt it when Dahlia hugged her. Sera was thankful for how close and tight the hug was, because without it, she was sure her buckling knees would send her crashing onto the floor. But the embrace came and went too fast. Sera wavered.

"You need to go," Dahlia said. Tears spilled down her face.

"What are you talking about?"

"The Western Fae Council is coming for you. You need to run, and never look back."

It was already too late. They were here. Their footsteps and voices echoed in the stairwell through the door.

"I'm sorry," Dahlia sobbed. "I tried to excuse myself sooner."

Before Sera could reach for the Wander Stone in her pocket, The Western Fae Council poured into the room with Lobelia at the head.

"The Southern Fae Council has deemed your case a conflict of interest and has relinquished the matter back to The Western Fae Council," Lobelia said.

Sera knew she was in for a difficult time. She prepared herself for the worst and bit back a cry as iron cuffs were slapped on her wrists. They glowed red hot like rings of fire against her skin. They absorbed her magic and burned it away, dampening her power and her energy, but not her resolve. She would not stop trying to save Vigo until it killed her, or worse, him.

"Let's go," Elder Lobelia said.

Everyone held a Wander Stone as they spoke their destination. By Elder Lobelia's hand, Sera was whisked away with them. In a breath, they arrived in the heart of the oak dense, Western Fae Woods.

Hunger

Vigo

Nearly a week had passed. Vigo spent that time hiding in the dark. As the hours turned into days, something sinister settled in him. It was a clawing sensation inside his gut, and a little voice that reminisced on how it felt to drink Jacob's blood. No matter how often Vigo tried, food never satiated the sharp hunger pains, and that voice he knew was his, had him dreaming of drinking blood again.

When people knocked at the door, Vigo curled into a ball on his bed and pulled the blankets over his head. *Like a child hiding from monsters in the night.* He smirked at the irony. For a week, Vigo waited, but Sera never showed. A new worry set in amongst his sinister desires. *What if something terrible happened to Sera?*

The sun hadn't yet set when Vigo made his way into town in a daze. Everything held a sense of familiarity without a sentiment of attachment. Peachy, sunset rays seared his skin, forming pussy blisters. There became a point when the pain meant nothing. It was just another sensation he experienced. He heard everything, smelled everything. The grass rustled beneath his shuffling feet. Dozens of heartbeats blurred together, and the faint smell of tobacco smoke permeated the air.

"Vi—" a man had started to say before Vigo pushed him against the building and drank deeply. The sun blisters healed and reformed in a euphoric cycle that lasted the entirety of his meal under the still setting sun.

The man was not enough to fill the void in Vigo's stomach. He needed more. Wanted more. Craved more. He licked the last drops of blood from his fangs and discarded the man's body like a simple apple core. He followed the thrum of heartbeats into the building. The air smelled sharp and sweet.

"You look like shit," a familiar voice said.

The room of patrons looked at Vigo, but their faces were nothing but blurry ovals to him. Vigo made his way to the man sitting nearest him at the bar top.

"What the hell happ—"

Thud, thud, crack.

In three swift motions Vigo had bridged the gap between them, broken the man's neck and forced his fangs into the soft flesh of his victim's throat

Someone screamed.

Glass shattered.

The blisters healed once again. In the shaded building, the wounds did not reappear.

A silver flash caught the corner of Vigo's eye just before a pointed blade was thrust into his back between his shoulders. The sharp pain tore Vigo away in a jolt. He pulled the dagger from his back. It clattered to the floor, and Vigo lunged for the man behind the counter. The tabletop was wet and sticky, but it barely registered as he toppled over the threshold. The man gripped a hanging chain. On the end of the chain, a lantern swung back and forth, right into Vigo's face. He tore it down, smashing it on the creaky, wooden floor. Hot oil splashed across Vigo's face. He recoiled in pain, baring his teeth. His shouts of agony melded into the patrons' screaming. The patrons abandoned the building as fire burned its way through the alcohol on the floor and up the side of the bar to the tabletop. The bartender didn't make it far. Vigo yanked him to the ground as the building caught fire around them. The heat from the fire was as stifling as the smoke that began filling the room. Vigo didn't care. He sunk his teeth into the bartender's neck and drank.

Flames closed in, and licked Vigo's skin like hot needles. The bartender's gurgled screams faded fast as Vigo feasted. Vigo had caught fire now, but it didn't matter. As soon as the fire had burned his flesh black, his curse healed him over.

Vigo left the bartender's corpse in a lifeless heap on the floor. Half the flesh on Vigo's face melted off as he walked out of the burning building. The once familiar faces of the townspeople rushed to the scene with buckets of water and dirt. A man of medium build stumbled around with a bottle in hand, and down he went. The bottle smashed with a mid-toned clunk as it hit the ground. Vigo saw the opportunity and lunged for it.

The man struggled feebly. He reeked of liquor and sweat, but he tasted like a dessert. All thick and sweet with fruity notes. The drunken man lifted his hand, clutching a broken bottle neck, and brought it down, jagged edge out, hard and fast into Vigo's shoulder. The glass broke off in his shoulder near his neck and collar bone.

The shards sawed at his flesh with every flex and movement. A hefty blow to his left temple threw him sideways. Dazed, he heard the man huff and crawl away in an awkward hobble. Out of the corner of his eye, he saw a woman frozen in fear. Vigo looked at her dead on, and her red bandana shined in the light of the burning building. Her eyes widened. Glittering tears fell down her soft features. She gripped a blood speckled board.

"Vig—"

Vigo grabbed the board and wrestled it away. It made a loud *thunk* as it hit the ground. The woman turned to run. Vigo grabbed her ankle, yanking her to the dirt. Her head smacked against the corner of the forgotten board. She was knocked unconscious, and Vigo got to fed unencumbered.

People stopped running towards the fire with dousing buckets. They ran away instead. The abandoned buckets served as obstacles for many fleeing amongst the smoky haze. A passerby tripped over a solid bucket filled to the brim with damp sand. Another lamb to the slaughter.

Clarity

Vigo

V igo's vision cleared. A man lay dying in his lap, bleeding out in the wake of the flames that continued to burn. A creak and sudden crack rang out. Down the street, the bar collapsed into a heap of smoldering splinters and ash. A waft of smoke whooshed into the sky, choking out the stars. The man in Vigo's lap flinched. His breathing was ragged.

"I'm—I'm so sorry," Vigo cried. He did it again.

He pulled the dying man to his chest. The man jolted and bit Vigo hard. He latched on so tightly that when Vigo shoved him away, he tore into his flesh. The man's lips were stained red, and blood seeped out of the bite on Vigo's arm. The dying man in his lap went silent. No breathing. No pulse.

Vigo heard another heartbeat. It was fast. A rustle of rock and debris startled him. He looked around to find Enzo hiding behind the town well.

"Is he dead?" The boy asked. His dark skin soaked up the firelight, turning him golden.

What is he still doing here?

The man in Vigo's lap clawed at him desperately, and Vigo looked down. The man's eyes were a crimson red, so dark they were almost black. He pulled himself upright, and when he opened his mouth, Vigo saw the fangs glint. Dread bottomed out his stomach, and if he had a heart, it would have skipped a beat as he realized what had happened.

"Run!" he yelled at Enzo.

Enzo listened and ran far and fast. Vigo slammed the man into the dirt, knees on his chest, hands around his neck. Tears welled in Vigo's eyes as he looked upon the beast writhing beneath him. The monster growled incoherently, baring its fangs. Red eyes glossed over in a frenzy. No matter how horrified, Vigo couldn't look away. "I'm sorry," he whispered because the horror he felt was nothing compared to the disgust. That's what he looked like; The grotesque thing he was grinding into the rubble?

He looked at the destruction around him. The devastation that he alone caused. An entire town felled in one night by a single monster. By him. He wished he had died *that* night. Everything he had been was gone or mutated into something unspeakable. He was a demonic parasite.

Vigo decided that he couldn't let another him exist. It was too dangerous. The man still struggled under Vigo's weight and crushing grip. "I'm sorry," Vigo said again. He picked up a brick, took a breath, and smashed it down on the man's head. He didn't die. Again, Vigo raised the brick above his head and brought it down on the man's skull. It took several blows, like a smith hammering a sword, before the man had no skull left to speak of. Just a lump of bloody flesh and shards of bone.

Vigo felt sick to his stomach. He scrambled away from the cooling corpse. He leaned against the well and remembered Enzo. He wanted to call out to him, to see if he was okay, but he also knew that he himself was the biggest danger. From the darkness and into the light of burning embers, Enzo crept back into sight.

"Stop," Vigo said, almost pleading.

Enzo stopped.

"What are you still doing here?" Vigo asked.

"Looking for you."

"You should be looking for your mother or ran to the next town like everyone else." Vigo couldn't help admonishing him. He knew he sounded angry, and he was, but not at Enzo.

"I found her." The tears on Enzo's cheeks caught the fire light.

"Oh..." Vigo finally noticed the red silk scarf tied around Enzo's neck. There was no mistaking it; it was Mia's. "Where is she?" He blurted it out without thinking.

Enzo pointed at an ash-covered lump in the distance.

Vigo hesitated. *Did I really?* He went to her. Enzo didn't follow. Not at first.

Vigo recoiled at the sight. Her temple was smashed open. Her eyes were grey, lifeless marbles without luster.

"What are you still doing here?" Enzo asked.

Vigo looked at Enzo. He was happy to have an excuse to look away from Mia. "I beat the monster off. It's gone for now."

Enzo was silent. His eyes were vacant.

"You should go see if you can catch up with anyone. Find safety in the next town."

"You didn't kill it, did you?"

"No. I don't think so."

Enzo crossed his arms. "Then I'm not leaving on my own."

Vigo sighed.

"I don't want it to get me. Everyone else ran or died, but you stayed. You ran it off. So, I'm staying with you."

"I—I..." Vigo stammered. He took a deep breath. Why didn't he just say he killed the monster? Then Enzo could have left and been fine. Now, he thought he was only safe with Vigo by his side. He couldn't have been further from the truth.

The boy was twelve and had never been scared of anything, except horses, and that was more a learned wariness. Thanks to Vigo, now he was terrified of standing still. Vigo could hear his heartbeat quicken the longer they stood there. Could Vigo keep it under control for just a couple days? Just until he got Enzo somewhere safe. Maybe they could send a message to another family member to care for him. It was risky.

"All right," Vigo said with a resigned sigh. "I'll take you to the next town."

"Okay."

His heartbeat quieted, but he was far from being calm. Enzo's steps were stiff, and he was silent as they walked together. They passed several dead bodies on their way out of town. Blood-soaked and dusted with dirt and ash. Vigo forced himself to look upon their faces. He couldn't remember what he did during his bloodthirsty frenzy, but he didn't exactly have to for him to figure it out. The carnage they walked amongst was enough of a vivid picture.

They reached the edge of the village, where the fires dwindled out. The homes were empty, nonetheless. Vigo wondered how long he was in the fugue state. Would the sun come up and disintegrate him? That would be a painfully long way to die. He could do it, though. Turn himself into his own pyre. Being burned alive was kinder than he deserved.

The little heartbeat and timid footsteps at his side gave him pause. He looked down at Enzo. who trudged alongside him. The boy was alone. He wasn't entirely safe with Vigo, but he had made it clear that he felt safe.

"Do you think the sun will be up soon?" Vigo asked.

"Maybe."

Maybe? That wasn't the answer Vigo wanted to hear. "Let's stop at my house and rest."

"I'm not going to sleep."

Vigo needed a place to hide from the sun if he was going to get Enzo to his family. Traveling by night was their only option right now, and it was too risky to keep going without being sure how much time had passed.

"Here," Vigo said. He gestured at his house. The dark curtains were still drawn, but to his surprise the kitchen window was broken. Why?

"I don't want to stop. I don't want to sleep. I want to get as far away from this place as possible. Far from it." Enzo protested.

Vigo wouldn't want to sleep either if he was Enzo. To be honest, Vigo wanted to put as much distance between them and the village, too.

"I know," he said. Vigo didn't want to play this card, partly because he would be lying, but it had to be done. "But can you do it for me? I'm getting kind of old compared to you, and that... that monster battle really took it out of me."

"You're not old," Enzo argued.

Vigo twisted the doorknob. Locked. He yanked on the door, and sharp pain shot through his shoulder. He grimaced. "I'm twenty-seven. That's more than double your age. Let an old man sit down, okay?" He yanked on the door again, busting the lock through the door frame and sending shooting pain through his shoulder, again. *What did I do to my shoulder?* He wondered.

"Why is your window broken," Enzo asked.

"I wish I knew," Vigo said.

The First Night
Vigo

E nzo stood on the doorstep. Vigo stepped inside. In the dark, he saw everything outlined clearly. The kitchen table, the matching chairs. Vigo hesitated to look down at the floor. He knew what was there. The smell of the stain permeated his nose and turned his stomach. It was probably nothing more than a brown mark on the floor now, and to anyone but him it wouldn't be a real concern. He took a deep breath, not because he needed to, but because the action itself was comforting. He was so used to breathing. He did it without even needing to. It just felt right. Normal even, and he needed any sense of normalcy he could hang onto.

Vigo was so busy in his own head, he forgot Enzo was right behind him. Enzo had followed him inside and let out a muffled "oof" against Vigo's back.

"What are you doing?" Enzo asked. He stepped around Vigo, brushing his arm as he passed. "I thought you needed to sit down. Why are you still stand—"

Vigo yanked Enzo back by his collar.

"You were about to trip on a chair. Stay here."

Vigo searched the cabinets for a matchbook and hoped an oil lamp or even a candle would appear next to it. He couldn't remember where he left the lantern, but there had to be a candle somewhere.

"Are you looking for these?" Enzo asked. He sat in a kitchen chair and held up a half-used candle and a matchbook.

"Where did you find those?" Vigo took the matches and the candle.

Enzo shrugged again. "They were on the table."

Vigo's first thought was that Sera might have stopped by. Maybe she was still there. "Sera!" he called.

No answer.

"Sera?"

Enzo shot up and out of his seat, tackling Vigo as he struggled to clap a hand over his mouth. He was too short.

"What are you doing?"

"What are *you* doing? Do you want that monster to hear you and come back for us?"

Enzo was right. Vigo hadn't been thinking like someone who had just survived a deadly encounter, let alone acting like someone who didn't wish to repeat the experience. Vigo was carrying on like he had nothing to fear, like he was the most dangerous predator in the vicinity. Unfortunately, that's because he was—Enzo just didn't know it yet. That didn't mean the two didn't share similar fears. Vigo still doubted it was a good idea to escort him to the next town. Those thoughts weren't helpful, though, so he set them aside.

If Sera had come home, she would be in their bedroom. "Stay here. I'll be right back," Vigo said.

"No."

"What?"

"I'm coming with you. I told you earlier, I'm scared."

Vigo sighed and picked up the candle and the matchbox. He struck the match and lit the candle. Enzo followed close behind up the narrow stairs.

"Do you think it got her?"

"No."

"But how do you know?"

Vigo didn't have a good answer. "I just do."

The two of them made their way to the bedroom. The door was shut, and Vigo's anticipation rose at the sight. He had waited days, maybe even weeks at this point, and she could be waiting for him just behind the door. That's when Vigo remembered why the matchbook and candle were on the kitchen table. The memory of Jacob's last hour flashed in his mind. The candle lit the room for them as Vigo hid from the sun. Jacob was eating the apple Vigo couldn't finish.

Enzo poked him in the back. "Why did you stop?"

Vigo grumbled an undiscernible response before reaching for the doorknob. He turned it, slow and precise. Click. The door popped open just a crack, and Vigo pushed it the rest of the way. The room was dark, except for the moonlight streaming in through the window, setting the bed in an ethereal glow. The bed was a mess, just like he left it. Sera wasn't here. Disappointment struck his chest and settled there.

"Why don't you lay down? Sleep a little bit," Vigo said.

"I'm not tired."

"You will be tomorrow."

"Yeah, but that's a problem for me tomorrow. Tonight, I have a monster to worry about."

"I promise it won't get you." While Vigo intended to keep his promise, there was still a sliver of doubt that pricked his skin.

Enzo plopped down on the bed and rested an arm on his knee. "And I promise I'm not sleeping."

He didn't. He was awake the whole night, but he was quiet. He stared out the window at what Vigo wondered. He hoped it was the beautiful moon and the twinkling stars and not the smoldering rubble of a village in the near distance. Vigo tried taking comfort in the moon. It didn't work. His gaze was drawn to the battlefield like a moth to the flame. Enzo's eyes appeared to gloss over as he stared. Had he fallen asleep with his eyes open?"

"You still awake?" Vigo asked.

"Yeah," Enzo said. He hadn't even glanced in Vigo's direction. Still fixated on the world outside.

Vigo swapped windows. He looked out at the one facing the orchard instead. While he wasn't sure what Enzo was looking for in the ruins of their home, Vigo knew he was looking for Sera. He imagined her blinking into existence at the edge of the orchard and rushing up to the house to him. But the longer he searched the tree line, the darker the orchard seemed. It was cast in grim shadows. It felt like an omen, and in that moment, Vigo knew that he would not be back, at least not for a very long time. If he ever did return, it would not be home.

He could dream all he wanted, but the fact was that Sera had left him and had not returned in nearly two weeks. At first, he had worried for her, but he knew she was capable of anything. Did she know he would become a monster? Is that why she left and never came back? Had she truly abandoned him? He started to think she had, and it tore his heart out. He clutched his chest and breathed deeply. He wanted to scream. He wanted to yell. He wanted to wail into the night. He couldn't. Not in front of Enzo. So, he held it in, all the heartache and anger.

He peeked over his shoulder at Enzo before grabbing a ball of twine from the bedside table drawer. It opened noisily, and Enzo's heartbeat jumped.

"What was that?" he asked.

Vigo took a moment. He steadied himself and said, "Just me."

Enzo settled back down, and after another glance over his shoulder, Vigo opened his pocketknife. It was a flimsy idea at best, and at worst, it wouldn't work, but it was something. He held the knife firmly against his neck, sharp edge pressing into the soft skin between his neck and jawline, securing its place with twine. If he opened his jaw to bite Enzo in a fury, the knife would puncture an important artery, and he would die, sparing Enzo's life. That's what he hoped anyway.

Stalemate

Sera

Elder Lobelia had Sera locked up in the Iron Bark Prison. It was a small forest of twisted, copper-colored trees. The forest had been cultivated near an iron-rich riverbed, permeating everything in the area with a pungent, metallic odor. The trees drank deeply and took on the orange coloring as every fiber was fused with the iron it took up with the water. There was no escape from a prison like this. Not for a fairy. Sera had been rendered powerless by her confines. She was always guarded, day and night, as if they feared she would perform another miracle by escaping an iron-tight prison with sheer will alone. She had tried. And failed.

For several days, she slept on the damp, ruddy dirt. It was warm to the touch, and if she dug her heels or hands below the surface, it scorched her skin in seconds. Food was brought to her three times a day. Breakfast, lunch, and dinner were flavorless, paltry morsels not befitting the word meal.

Late one evening, Sera received a visitor. Dahlia sat on her knees opposite her. The earthen cage separated them.

"I'm so sorry," Dahlia said.

Her apology settled uncomfortably in the air. What was Sera supposed to say? 'It's okay,' or 'I forgive you'? Or even, 'don't worry, I'm fine'? All of those would have been lies.

"I heard that you might get one more hearing," Dahlia said.

"They won't listen anyway." Sera's best chance was with the Southern Fae Council. That chance was gone.

"I can persuade them. Two is easier than four."

"Two, who I assume already told Elder Lobelia it was perfectly fine to kill my husband as punishment. They would never help me save him, even if he is still alive." Too many days had passed since she left Vigo in Jacob's care. Hope of his survival waned.

"Forget him for one moment, please." Dahlia's doe eyes glistened. She reached between the small gaps in the winding barrier between them, her wrist knocking into a branch, turning red from its touch. Her hand closed around Sera's. "You need to worry about yourself. How can you save yourself now? How can you lessen another punishment they are surely debating now?"

Sera hadn't considered her fate past Vigo's. "If he dies, I would rather run an iron blade right through my heart than live without him."

Dahlia sighed with indignance and squeezed Sera's hand so tight it hurt. "How did you get like this?"

"You were once happy for me," Sera said. "But after you got promoted... I hadn't heard from you in months."

"I didn't think anything of it. Months to us are like minutes for humans."

"Not for me. Not anymore," Sera said. She treasured those months. Those happy few years she was allowed to spend with Vigo.

"I thought...I thought I taught you well enough."

"What's that supposed to mean?"

"I had hoped he was merely an experience, a fun time to look back on and appreciate. I thought your love for him was as fleeting as his mortal life. I didn't realize you or the Elders would take it this far."

"And I thought I could get away with it. I guess we were both wrong."

A heavy silence passed between them.

"I beg you, please think of yourself. Ask for leniency, and I'll do what I can to plea on your behalf."

Dahlia was trying, but Sera warred with herself about whether it was too little too late.

"I can't promise anything."

"I understand."

The downturn twitch at the corners of Dahlia's mouth and the slight furrow in her brows she failed to hide showed Sera a different story. Dahlia gave Sera's hand another squeeze. It was lighter, softer, more loving, and forlorn. Sera believed Dahlia would help her all she could despite not approving of her life choices. That's what loved ones do for each other, after all.

"Thank you," Sera said.

Dahlia pulled back her hand. She rubbed her injured wrist as she gave Sera one last look and a sad smile before departing.

Vigo's Remorse
Vigo

Enzo was right; he stayed up the whole night. Vigo did, too. He discreetly put the knife back in his pocket, and the twine in the drawer. The sky blended like watercolor from the deep violet of night to the peachy morning sunrise. Vigo hid under a dark blanket. He pulled it over his head like a hooded cloak. Enzo came and sat next to him. He stifled a laugh.

"What are you doing?" He asked.

"When I was sick, I developed a severe sun sensitivity." It wasn't a lie, but it wasn't exactly the truth.

He was warm under the thick, dark wool. He was too warm in fact, but sacrifices had to be made. It seemed that's what his new life was about. Simply living a miserable existence for the sake of living. He contemplated what to do about it. The sun could and would definitely kill him, given the chance. He just had to withstand the agonizing pain for probably forty-five minutes at least.

He seriously considered it. The experience would be literal torture, but if it meant he wasn't a threat to anyone again, that outcome would be worth that sacrifice. For now, though, all he could do was fantasize and dread his planned demise. He promised Enzo he would help him. He intended to keep that promise. After that, he could experiment with all kinds of ways to kill himself. *Would Sera care if he died now?* He wondered. He shook the thought away.

"Sleep well?" Vigo teased.

Enzo smirked. "I told you I wouldn't."

"You'll crash eventually."

"Maybe."

"Crashing isn't good for you, by the way."

"It's better than being dead."

"Fair point." Vigo shrugged. "Are you hungry yet?"

Enzo perked up and swung his legs over the edge of the bed. "Depends, what's there to eat?"

"This is a farm. You have options."

"And those are?"

"Come down and see."

Vigo descended the farmhouse's narrow stairway, with Enzo practically stepping on his heels on their way down. Enzo pushed past him at the bottom of the stairs. He rushed over to the kitchen window to pull the drapes open. Vigo flinched; light flooded the room in a wistful way. It gave him a throbbing headache and made his eyes painfully warm and itchy. Aside from his personal discomfort, everything was calm—peaceful, even—in the soft morning light. A nest of baby birds above the kitchen window outside chirped excitedly. Sera loved the nest. It had hosted several bird families in the past three years. Especially the snow sparrows who stayed for the winter. Vigo remembered the other day when they sheared the sheep and how the birds of the orchard greeted them for scrap tufts of fluff. It was only a couple weeks ago, but it felt so much longer.

Enzo zipped around the room, opening cupboards and drawers in his search for breakfast. five apples sat on the table in a pile. After they left, no one was going to be eating the food, and Enzo would need to eat during their trip. From the pantry, Vigo pulled down a picnic basket lined with embroidered dishcloths his mother had sewn.

"Grab everything you want to eat for the road, and I'll help you put it in here," Vigo said as he flipped open the basket lid. The hinges groaned, but Vigo was sure only he could hear that.

Enzo's arms were full of treats that spilled onto the table when he sat down. There were nuts, raisins, sheep jerky, bread, and even a small cheese round. The boy crunched on oblong nuts between bites of apple, and between mouthfuls, he asked, "Why aren't you eating? This is your food."

"I'm not hungry," Vigo lied.

Enzo shrugged and went back to eating.

Vigo was hungry. Not very, but enough to be concerning. There was an empty feeling in him the size of a cherry pit. He could wait to eat, but should he, and for how long? Maybe it would be best if he slunk off by himself to catch something fresh and hopefully filling enough to keep him satisfied. The only obstacle stopping him would be Enzo. He was very attached. No one could blame the kid, though. He lost his mother and his home all in one night. He thought maybe he put the knife away a bit too soon, but he also knew Enzo would ask questions if he saw it.

As Enzo enjoyed his food, Vigo recalled that not all the spring apples had been picked. Enzo loved climbing the apple trees to pick the fruit. He was good at it, too. Vigo had been climbing the apple trees since he was a boy, and the only one who matched him in climbing was Enzo. *It would be nice to do that again,* Vigo thought.

Once Enzo had finished his food, Vigo helped him pack it up by rewrapping the cheese in a fresh, dry cloth. Out of the corner of his eye, he caught Enzo's sour expression as he packed the jar of nuts and dried berries.

"Everything all right?" Vigo asked.

"She loved picnics," Enzo whispered to himself.

Vigo didn't need to ask. He knew Enzo was talking about Mia. She did love picnics. Once a month in the spring, summer, and fall, Enzo and his parents would have a day trip to the base of the mountains. After Enzo's father died in the accident, Enzo wouldn't go. That was until Vigo and Sera started joining them for their picnics.

Vigo finished wrapping the cheese and went to place it inside the basket. An idea came to mind when he laid eyes on the metal flask tucked neatly in the corner, next to a water skin. He swapped the flask out with the cheese and shoved it into his pocket.

"Why don't we go apple picking before we leave?" Vigo suggested.

Enzo's mood seemed to immediately improve at the idea. "How many?" he asked.

"As many as you can carry."

Enzo slammed the basket lid shut before taking off towards the door.

"As many as YOU can carry!" Vigo repeated himself.

Enzo stopped still as soon as he opened the door. Vigo heard the kid's heart skip a beat before he smelled the smoke waft into the room.

Enzo kept his gaze fixed on the outside. "Where do you think it is now?" He asked.

Vigo knew *it* was the monster from last night. *It* meant him. "I have a pretty good idea. But we should be fine. Do you want me to go first?"

"Yeah."

Vigo eyed the coat closet to the left. He ducked down and squeezed inside. It was pitch black. The light streaming in through the kitchen window couldn't reach him in the closet. It was nice.

Enzo snorted a laugh from the other side. "What are you doing?"

"I'm—" Vigo let the blanket fall to the ground. "—trying to—" he struggled to put on one of the cloaks he found hanging in the closet. "—change my sun protection."

"Okay." Enzo sounded amused.

On Vigo's way out of the closet, his foot caught on the blanket. He sighed. "Okay," he said, freeing his foot with a shake.

"Are you ready?" Vigo asked.

Enzo's brows drew together, and he smiled. "Are you?"

As ready as can be expected, Vigo thought.

He slipped around Enzo. Looking at the sun-kissed outside made him dizzy as he stepped out into it. The cloak seemed to work— for now. The first row of apple trees and shady reprieve wasn't far from the house. Enzo followed close behind as Vigo led the way with a throbbing head.

Once they were under the apple canopy, Vigo's headache subsided. Enzo began climbing a tree almost immediately. Vigo took a minute to think and leaned against the tree.

"Stay close," Enzo called down.

If Vigo's plan was going to work, he needed to not be close to Enzo. "Then how am I supposed to pick apples?"

"I didn't think you were."

Above, leaves rustled, and a twig snapped. Vigo looked up to see Enzo holding a spring apple in one hand.

"Catch!" Enzo shouted just before an apple hit the ground with a hard *thump.*

"Maybe you should have taken the basket with you," Vigo pointed out.

"Then pass it up."

Vigo did, and it made him smile.

Enzo moved on to another tree. Only a few apples could be picked at a time from the tree. It was a rule Sera put in place. Harvests were smaller not because the trees weren't healthy but because Sera advocated for nature. Don't over pick. Don't collect extra water. Don't waste. The orchard was the healthiest it had ever been. By leaving fruit behind, animals, bugs, and pollinators flourished.

A family of chittering squirrels played tag somewhere. Bees hummed in the distance. Songbirds romanced each other. Vigo was sure only he could hear all that, but Enzo could probably at least hear the birds. Vigo knew how lively the orchard was, but he never experienced it like this. Every sound, every scent, was easy to take in. The calm atmosphere of today was such a stark contrast to last night.

Somehow, in this moment, life was the most vibrant it had ever been for him. That was until he remembered what it had cost him. His newfound vibrance in the world was fleeting. It was too tainted for him to remain fond of. He didn't give it another kind thought, especially while that pit in his stomach darkened with need. He was suddenly overwhelmed by all he heard. The loudest sound was that of a bell, like a cacophony of chimes in a windstorm.

It took Vigo longer than he would like to admit for him to figure out what it was. The tolling bell was breakfast, lunch, and dinner for however long Vigo could make it last. He didn't even have to seek it out because Millie, the white and black goat, came trotting up to him. The scene was perplexing; Millie didn't like him. Then he realized it wasn't him she was after. She was after her breakfast.

It was about that time, and Vigo hadn't tended to any of the animals in days. He had forgotten about them, and it seemed that most of them had no problem wandering off to find food. Maybe they caught the eyes of the fleeing townspeople and were taken. He hoped that whatever happened to them, they were happy. Someone should be.

"Millie!" Enzo shouted. He jumped down. His knees buckled as he hit the ground.

Vigo stopped him from falling with a quick fist full of his shirt. The kid steadied himself against the tree before scratching Millie on the head. She bopped her nose against the basket of goodies.

Vigo's stomach churned at the thought he had mere moments ago. The image of him draining life from Millie was hard to push away. Sure, they didn't get along, but she had personality, and she trusted him to care for her. She stayed despite the lack of stable meals the past week.

"Give her all the apples she wants," Vigo said.

Before Enzo could finish pulling an apple from the basket, Millie snatched it away to mull it over. Her chomps sent juice squirting. Vigo pulled an apple out of the basket and slipped it into his pocket. He was keeping it safe for later.

"Looks like I have to pick more," Enzo said.

"Then you better get to it."

While Enzo foraged for another armful of apples, Vigo was left alone with his thoughts. He had options. He could drink the goat dry and cook the rest of her. No waste. He gave Millie an apologetic look. "I'm sorry," he whispered to her. The breeze shifted. It carried a hint of ash that had Vigo's head turn towards town. He had another option. Stale food. Someone already dead. Less of a waste that way. He swallowed hard. Saliva pooled in his mouth at just the thought of drinking even cold blood. He really needed to eat, and soon.

"Enzo?" He called out. "There's something I need to do. I'll be back."

"Wait, where are you going?" Enzo leaped out of the tree and hit the ground running.

"Not far."

Enzo yanked on Vigo's cloak. "You can't leave me alone."

"You won't be alone. You have Millie."

"No." Vigo took a deep breath. It was then he realized he hadn't been breathing all this time. He didn't need to breathe anymore. He was still taken aback by how nice it felt. How familiar it was to breathe. It almost made him feel normal again. Almost.

"I need to do something, and you can't come," Vigo continued. "You're worried about that monster coming back, right?"

"Yeah."

"What I have to do is going to help keep that thing away."

"You promise?"

"I promise." Vigo offered his pinky finger. "And I promise I'll be right back."

"Okay."

The deal was sealed with a pinky swear. Enzo didn't go back to climbing a tree. He sat in the grass with Millie instead. He fed her another apple and hugged her close. Vigo resisted the urge to ruffle the kid's curls before he left. He would be lying if he said it was easy to leave Enzo with tear-filled eyes. Vigo's determination to keep Enzo safe from himself was the only thing keeping him from turning around. He imagined embracing Enzo, wiping his tears away, and telling him that he wasn't going after all.

Two houses had burned to the ground overnight, along with the bar. From the outside, one of the houses made of brick looked fine, aside from the missing roof and scorch marks. Three distinct bodies, covered in ash, lay lifeless in the road. Vigo was drawn to Mia. Last night, he couldn't bring himself to look at her. Now, he knew he owed her at least that much.

Her head rested near a blood-splattered board. Fine ash clung to her skin and hair. Dried blood crusted over her temple and trailed down her jawline. His gaze fell on her neck. He needed to know if her death was just an accident brought on by the chaos of last night or if he had done it. With trembling hands, he clumsily brushed the ash from her neck. His eyes locked onto the bite mark, and it brought him back to the one he left on Jacob. They were a near exact match. He couldn't even fool himself into some delusion that an animal passing by just decided to try a nibble. *I should bring her back,* he thought. Mia had the right to a funeral, just like Jacob. Just like everyone Vigo killed, but Vigo was thinking pragmatically. He only had the time for one funeral. He needed to get Enzo somewhere safe. Somewhere with someone who could take of him.

Vigo promised he would be back as soon as possible. He refused to consciously drink any more of Mia's blood. It wouldn't be right. Drinking anyone's blood wasn't 'right.' But that dark pit in his stomach reminded him what would happen if he didn't, so he sought out someone else.

Not far from Mia was another familiar face. His ankle was twisted to the side and most likely broken. It was the village doctor. The wire stems of his glasses were bent, and the glass cracked like a spider's web. His bag of medical supplies spilled out. He intended to help people, even as he feared for his own life.

Vigo pushed against the nagging feeling that it was wrong. He didn't have any more time to waste. While he debated morals, Enzo was waiting. If he wasn't crying, he was at least fighting back the urge. He was probably too terrified to make any noise that might bring the monster right to him. The irony that Enzo was crying for the monster to save him from the monster wasn't lost on Vigo. He didn't find it amusing. He found it sickening to the point of overbearing guilt. The weight of that guilt was sure to only gain.

As he looked into the man's decaying eyes, he told himself that's all it was. A dead guy. He didn't believe the lie. He couldn't. Not while the dead guy was once a man he knew.

Vigo sighed as he knelt towards the man's exposed neck. It was gritty with dust and dirt and ash that scraped against his tongue as he drank. The man smelled like beer. His blood was cool and thick like jelly and bore the aftertaste of stale bread. He must have been drinking at the bar before it caught fire.

Vigo told himself that the doctor's death wasn't just meaningless slaughter. Vigo was going to make him last—for Enzo. It didn't comfort him as much as he had hoped. But repeating the phrase several times in his head was a good distraction while he drank. It drew his attention away from the disgusting act.

When he had finished, Vigo took the flask from his pocket and popped the cap. He went back in for another drink. He didn't swallow. Vigo let the blood fill his mouth and spit the contents into the flask. The process made him feel like a dirty, disease-ridden animal sick beyond saving.

"That's because you are," he whispered to himself.

Once it was full, he pocketed the flask and wiped his mouth. Blood smear marred the back of his hand, so he licked it off with a grimace. He had made Enzo wait long enough. Probably too long.

Vigo left the doctor to return to Mia's side. Carefully, he picked her up with an arm under her knees and the other around the back of her shoulders. His own shoulder screamed for him to drop her. Three points of stabbing pain shredded flesh deep within his shoulder. He ignored it as best he could. With the dead weight of a lost loved one, he headed home. It was weird to call it that. The orchard was home only in memory. The town was deserted, and Sera was still gone.

Did Sera know what he would become? Is that why she left? She loved him enough to save his life, but she couldn't love the monster she knew he would become. He didn't blame her for not loving him anymore. However, he did blame her for what she made him. Why even save his life at that point? He would be better off dead. A stolen eternity wasn't worth living.

As he walked, Mia's twists swung like tall grass in the breeze, and her dangling legs weighed heavier on the other side. He kept his gaze straight ahead in the direction of the orchard. He returned to find

Enzo still holding Millie close, but they had changed spots. They sat under an apple tree. The moment Vigo saw Enzo, Enzo must have seen him, too. The boy left Millie behind in a desperate run.

Vigo laid Mia in the grass and stepped over her. Enzo barreled into Vigo. Enzo threw his arms around him like a vice. Not needing to breathe was suddenly beneficial.

"Thank you," Enzo whispered.

"For what?"

"For coming back."

Vigo's heart sank to know that there was at least a small part of Enzo that believed Vigo wouldn't return.

Enzo finally let go. His eyes were puffy, but it was hard to tell if that was from the silent tears the kid probably shed or the fact that he hadn't slept yet.

"Let's go sit," Vigo suggested. He was keenly aware of the fact that they had been hugging in broad daylight away from the shady refuge of the orchard canopy. He was also aware of the fact that he was only being shielded by a cloak.

Vigo nudged Enzo towards the shade, where they sat side by side. Millie plopped down on the other side of Enzo. For whatever reason, she seemed content munching on the ankle-high grass not far from the patch of moss they sat on. She stretched her neck out as far as she could to pluck the greens without getting up.

"Let's wait a while here. Decide what we want to do next."

Enzo was silent.

"I'm sorry about your mother," Vigo said.

"Thank you for bringing her back."

"What kind of service do you think she would like?"

"I think she would like to be buried next to the rose bush with Dad."

There was a pink rose bush near Enzo's house. His parents planted it the day they got married.

"When the sun sets, I'll get started," Vigo said.

"Aren't you afraid that thing will come back by then?"

It hurt Vigo to hear Enzo call him a thing and a monster. What hurt more, though, was how accurate the names were.

"I promise, that"—Vigo struggled with the word—"creature won't get you tonight or anytime soon." He wrapped an arm around Enzo and pulled him close. He wasn't sure who needed the affectionate gesture more, him or Enzo. Vigo settled into the divots of the tree and laid his head back. Enzo laid his head on Vigo's shoulder. For a few hours, their lives hadn't fallen apart. A sense of peace settled in the fruity-scented air that lulled them to sleep.

Ritual Rites
Vigo

V igo jammed the shovel head into the dirt and sighed. His shoulder was numb from the pain of use. Something was definitely stuck in there. He had just finished digging Mia's grave. Her lifeless body was rolled up in a cotton bedsheet near him on the ground. He stood in the pit six feet deep, eyes level with Mia's form. He had avoided looking at her until now. Now that her grave had been dug. Vigo glanced at her husband's tombstone, a small boulder with quarts inclusions, and the robust rose bush that guarded the site. Its thorny tines bowed with fragrant buds just shy of full bloom. A door slammed shut, and moments later, Enzo appeared.

"Need help?"

"I might."

Vigo handed the shovel to Enzo, who discarded it, seemingly without thought. Enzo sat in the grass, bracing his heels as he offered Vigo a hand or two. Vigo gripped Enzo's forearms as he climbed the crumbling dirt wall. With a lot of effort, some clumsy maneuvering, and Enzo's help, Vigo crawled out of the grave with gritted teeth as his shoulder threatened to give out on him. It throbbed as he laid out on the grass. Dirt dusted his hands and tickled his nose.

"Thanks," he said.

"Yeah."

Sullen silence filled the space between them and broke against the humming nightlife. Scattered in the dewy grass was a stout candle, a matchbox, a book, and a bowl of chocolate drops, gleaming in the moonlight. Mia had a sweet tooth. Vigo couldn't imagine Enzo offering anything else at her funeral.

"Are you ready?" Vigo asked.

Enzo's glossy eyes reflected a sliver of moon. "I don't think I can do it." He looked away.

Vigo's eyes darted from Enzo to Mia, to the grave, and back to Enzo. He and Sera really made a mess of everything. Sera's absence, especially now, made it clear to Vigo: she could get along fine without him. The same couldn't be said for Vigo. She should have let him die. He wished she had. It would have been a much better fate than cursing him to live, only to leave him for dead anyway.

Vigo sighed softly as he rose. "You don't have to." He went to Mia and knelt next to her. "Close your eyes," he said to Enzo. "And plug your ears. Don't look or listen until I tap you on the shoulder."

Enzo did as he said, and with less effort than expected, Vigo pushed Mia over. He rolled her into the grave. An unceremonious thump boomed in his ears that brought tears to his eyes. They welled up like the orchard stream after a rainstorm: too rapid and full to damn up. He wiped his tears with fruitless effort. More readily spilled over as he made his way back to Enzo and tapped him on the shoulder.

Enzo hugged him tight, squeezing. If he wasn't a kid, Vigo was sure Enzo's grip would be enough to break bones. He wondered what it would be like to die that way. For him to be crushed into a lump of tender meat and shards of bone. 'Unpleasant, but deserved' was all that came to mind.

"Let's go," he said.

Enzo took up the shovel. Vigo was sure it was a burden to carry, but he wasn't going to let Enzo back out. He knew Enzo would never forgive himself if he didn't at least do this.

Burying Mia was agonizingly slow. It took nearly all night to dig the grave itself, so Vigo wasn't surprised when the sun rose before they were done. Spade by spade, they took turns filling Mia's grave with dirt and tears. They could have easily pushed the pile of soil over the edge and been done with it, but that would have been disrespectful. Honoring someone's life meant honoring their death with your time. Time was slowed by mourning despair. Rushing through the process was a sign of trying to forget as soon as possible.

The ones you love deserve to be remembered. Guilt made Vigo's heart twinge at the thought. He remembered how he burned Jacob in the fire pit. How he abandoned his remains mixed amongst the wood ash. Vigo didn't even bother burying him. He should have given Jacob at least that much dignity in death.

By the time Mia's grave was complete, the sun had risen to midday, and Vigo suffered red, rashy blisters on his hands, lower cheeks, and chin.

"What happened?" Enzo asked when he finally noticed.

Vigo winced as he brushed a peeling thumb across an exceptionally large blister on the backside of his hand. "Sunburn."

Enzo inspected his own hands and arms. He even patted his face. "I'm not burnt."

"It seems I'm much more susceptible than you."

Enzo's brows knitted tighter in confusion. "But you're always in the sun, and I've never seen you burn this bad before."

Vigo let his hands fall to his sides. "It's new for me, too."

Enzo stared at Vigo in silence. He seemed unconvinced.

"Don't worry about it. Let's finish this," Vigo said.

Enzo set up the votive candle and the bowl of chocolate drops at the foot of Mia's grave. Vigo stood a pace back as he watched Enzo kneel in front of the altar. He struck the match and lit the candle.

"Mom?" he said.

Vigo's nerves were figuratively and literally on fire. His hands and face itched. Bloody skin clung to the undersides of his nails after he scratched his chin.

"Mom. I miss you," Enzo continued.

The candle flame flickered.

"I was hoping..." His voice cracked. "I was hoping we could eat some chocolate together again, and we could finish that book we were reading."

The flame winked out and then roared to life again with a power much greater than that of a candle wick. The air thickened with the presence of Mia's spirit. For Vigo, it was a stifling presence. He swallowed hard to clear the lump in his throat. It didn't work. He knew the spirits of the departed could only listen. He still had the irrational fear that Mia would somehow find a way to tell Enzo that, like a rabid animal, he had killed her without a second thought.

One by one, Enzo ate the chocolate drops. He sobbed between bites as he read aloud. It was a book about a pirate and a prince. A forbidden love story with a happy ending. Every pained sound Enzo made squeezed Vigo's heart. Part of him really wished it would crush his heart. Maybe then he would die.

"I love you," Enzo said to his mother. "I miss you and dad, but..." He wiped his tears. "I'll keep going. I'll be okay. I still have Vigo."

The guilt Vigo carried in his chest was unbearably heavy. He had to sit. He was the reason all this was happening. He deserved to die. He wanted to die, but he couldn't. Enzo needed him. Vigo pulled on his hair and bit his tongue. Blood pooled in his mouth. The coppery taste disgusted him. It was another reminder of what he did. It would have been all too easy to spit it out. To run and hide away in a dark corner. He swallowed it. He kept it with him. What he had done. Never forget. Never forgive. He composed himself. Enzo couldn't see him falling apart.

The chocolate was gone, and Enzo said his goodbyes. When he did, the candle faded out to a smoking glow that went dark, too.

To Nurture

Vigo

At dusk the next day, Vigo approached Enzo with a question. "Did your mother have a sister?" He asked.

"No. Why?"

Vigo didn't know how to approach the subject delicately. "You're going to need someone to take care of you, preferably a family member."

"You're like family."

The statement felt very offhand, and yet heartfelt nonetheless. "But I'm not your family. Isn't there someone else you know, like an uncle, who could take care of you? I'm sure they're going to be worried once word of what happened here reaches them."

"What would you do if I didn't?"

"But you do, right?"

"I mean, yeah...but hypothetically, what would you do?"

"Hypothetically, I wouldn't know what to do with you. It would take me some time to figure out."

"Oh…" The atmosphere shifted, and something felt very off, very suddenly. "Well, it's a good thing I have an uncle then."

"What's his name?"

"Da… Daniel."

"Where is he?"

"Do you have a map?"

"I can draw one." Vigo drew a very rough map in the dirt. He doubted Enzo could read it because he swore that if he wasn't the one to draw it, he wouldn't have been able to decipher what all the awkward squiggles were.

"What's that?" Enzo pointed to a poorly drawn, fat fish with mismatched fin sizes on the eastern side of the 'map.'

"That's Port Haddock. It's quite a hike. Almost three weeks straight from here."

"That's it!" Enzo said. "We don't get to visit him very often."

"I don't think I've ever heard of you visiting an Uncle Daniel."

Enzo crossed his arms and shrugged his shoulders. "He works too much because he's single."

The trip would take roughly a month. Give or take a few days to a week. At best, they would travel at night, and at worst, under the sun and on foot. Not to mention they couldn't trek straight from the orchard to the coast. They would need to resupply at a halfway point, and hopefully, Vigo could make sure Enzo got a good night's sleep in a real bed at a tavern or an inn. Realistically, it would be four weeks in total. Vigo hoped they could find a caravan route and hitch a ride. The sooner Enzo was under his uncle's care, the better.

Vigo, Enzo, and Millie traveled by night along the river flowing from the mountains, through the orchard, and out of town. It would take them close enough to see Lloydstone before flowing into a lake near the city entrance.

Enzo walked close to Vigo, almost too close. Enzo's heartbeat was steady and strong in Vigo's ears. Vigo clutched the flask in his pocket, resisting the urge to take a drink. He had to conserve it as best he could. He told himself to wait. Wait until sunrise, but another part of him longed to drink it down in one gulp. He focused on the sky above instead. The full moon and bright stars lit the way, illuminating the rushing river with silver light, like a path of celestial light guiding them toward a better tomorrow.

The view was distracting enough for some time, but eventually, Enzo's blood coursing in his veins was too loud for Vigo to ignore, and that was dangerous. He took a drink. Then another. He let it linger on his tongue as he swallowed slowly to savor, to satiate, to trick himself into believing that he drank more than he really had. Disgust for himself sent a shiver down his spine.

"What are you drinking?" Enzo asked.

"Wine," Vigo lied. He paused, set the basket he carried down, and dug out the water skin. "You should drink this instead."

Enzo gulped it down. Drops dribbled down his chin when he stopped to gasp for air.

"Careful," Vigo said. "If you were that thirsty, you should have said something a while ago."

Enzo wiped his face on his sleeve and laughed. "I didn't realize how thirsty I was."

"Don't forget to fill it back up."

Enzo didn't. He dipped it in the river and let the water skin fill to the brim before corking.

They walked on with Millie trotting close by, creating a cacophony of disjointed jingles. After a while, the sky changed from dark blue hues to soft lavender streaks. The moon appeared to fade, and the shine of the stars dulled. Sunrise was coming, so Vigo flipped up his hood and waited anxiously for the sun to crest the horizon. When it did, he kept his head downcast. The weight of his guitar slung across his chest and over his good shoulder shifted to his lower back. Enzo yawned, and his pace noticeably slowed.

"Let's stop here until nightfall," Vigo said.

Enzo lounged on the ground. He tied his mother's red silk scarf around his head to keep his dark curls from snagging on the grass and pulled the extra fabric over his eyes. Vigo pressed his palms into his forehead and groaned. His sun headache was setting in for the day. It was a dull thumping that grew stronger as the day wore on. When the sun peaked, Vigo was rattled from the feeling of his skull being beaten on like a festival drum.

Vigo squirmed his way to a shady spot in the open plains sparsely populated by young trees. Millie rolled in the muddy riverbank, kicking up sludgy water. Vigo would be lying if he said the thought hadn't crossed his mind, but then he would be wet and muddy for hours. He decided that it wasn't worth it.

When the sky mellowed into a dusty rose, Vigo's headache subsided. It was more tolerable as the day moved into evening. He took that rare time between day and night to play. He tested the strings, and not to his surprise, the chords were out of tune. He plucked and strummed the strings, and twisted the tuning pegs until the chords sounded just right. He saved E string for last. It was picky, and easily snapped if not done just right. He winced every time he had to adjust it.

The familiar ache in his shoulder intensified as he played a delicate tune, and Enzo finally stirred. He pulled the scarf from his head and tied it back around his neck. Clumsy from sleep, he walked over to Vigo and plopped down next to him.

"What are you playing?"

Vigo continued the melody without needing to spare much concentration as he said, "Echoes of the Seasons." The song gradually changed from its low, somber pitch to a mid-range accented with a quick succession of three high-pitched notes that mimicked clinking glass. "This part is called Winter Chimes."

Enzo leaned in, his shoulder pressing into Vigo's arm as he played. His eyes trailed every movement Vigo made. "Can you teach me?"

Vigo stopped playing. Enzo looked not at Vigo but at his guitar, his gaze unblinking. His hands on his knees twitched. He really wanted to try. Learning guitar took practice, and practice took time. Time Vigo didn't have. If Vigo started Enzo on the path to music, he would not be there to see him through it and watch him grow. It would be cruel, but to whom, exactly, Vigo wasn't sure. Maybe to both of them in equal measure, but maybe, if Enzo truly enjoyed playing, Vigo could gift him his guitar as a goodbye present. It would be the last meaningful thing Vigo could do for a kid who deserved the world. Vigo couldn't give Enzo the world, but he could give him that.

"All right." Vigo's mouth quirked up on its own. "Sit on your butt and cross your legs."

Enzo did.

Vigo handed him the guitar. "Hold it steady," he said.

He went on to teach Enzo the anatomy of the guitar. Enzo touched every piece with an awestruck gleam in his eyes. Vigo wasn't sure how much he was retaining, but it made him happy. Enzo's happiness was contagious, and it filled Vigo's chest with mirthful laughter as he watched Enzo strum the strings awkwardly.

"Here, try this." Vigo helped Enzo adjust his form. "Is that more comfortable?"

"Yep!"

"Good. Now, try this." Vigo instructed Enzo on how to play several chords in a specific order to create a simple, repeating tune. It was one of the first patterns Vigo had learned when he first tried to play.

Enzo's timing between chords was uneven and unsure, but his enthusiasm never waned. When the darkness crept in, and the guitar was near impossible to see clearly, they packed up again and moved on.

Troubled Rain

Vigo

For the past week, they had done everything backward. They travelled at night and slept during the day, but it seemed to be working out for both of them. Walking around in broad daylight and trying to keep all his skin covered wasn't easily done for Vigo, and Enzo could only sleep during the day.

Grey clouds blocked the sun, lessening Vigo's headache. He intently watched the handful of nuts and dried fruit he had set out. He hoped to catch a fat raccoon, or a rabbit. A squirrel would have even been welcome. His flask was running low on blood.

"I'm watching you," Vigo said.

Millie trotted towards the pile of goodies carefully placed on a concealed net trap made from strips of green, woody plants and baby trees. He would be lying if he said the thought of eating Millie hadn't crossed his mind again. He wasn't the only one with low rations. The picnic basket was running low, too.

An arm's reach from Vigo, Enzo pulled his knees to his chest, squeezing himself ever smaller and tighter. He shivered. With the gloomy cloud cover, it was an unusually cool spring day.

"Here," Vigo said. He shrugged his cloak off his shoulders and put it around Enzo.

"Don't you need it?"

"I'm not cold," Vigo said.

Vigo gestured for Enzo to snuggle up. He knew he wasn't going to warm anyone up, but physical touch seemed to be of great importance for Enzo. Vigo sang a soothing lullaby. His own mother used to sing it to him as a kid. It was called, "The Ballad of Stars".

It didn't take long before Enzo's head thumped against Vigo's shoulder. His mouth hung open as he slept. Vigo imagined how dry and sore his throat would be when he woke. Tenderly, he placed an index finger under Enzo's chin and closed his mouth before eyeing the trap he had set.

The empty feeling inside made him fidgety and irritable. He took the lid off his flask and indulged in the coppery smell that wafted up. It did little to satiate his cravings, but at least it kept him sane. His sanity mattered the most right now. The sore throat didn't bother him much anymore, and while it was excruciating, he didn't care that his stomach twisted in knots like it was tangled in barbed wire. Enzo felt safe with him. Most importantly. Enzo was safe from him as long as he could ignore the pain. He would rend his own flesh if that's what it took to keep Enzo safe.

A cold gust rustled the treetops, and the noisy pitter-patter of rain battered the leafy canopy. Rain plummeted into the river hard and fast. Hefty droplets dripped off the foliage above and onto Vigo's head. The cold sensation permeated his scalp. Enzo stirred on Vigo's shoulder, wiping the water from his eyes.

Vigo pulled Enzo to stand and pointed. "To the base of the tree," he said.

Millie beat them to it with her bell ringing furiously as her stubby, black-and-white legs galloped the whole way there. They stood under the tree, watching steam rise from the earth. A misty haze fell over the land as it swelled with water.

"My shoes are wet," Enzo complained.

"Mine too." Worse than squishy socks, though, was watching Enzo shiver next to him. As if that weren't enough, the noise was nearly agonizing. He pressed the palms of his hands to his ears.

Rainy afternoons were once a soothing sleep inducer. Now, they were overwhelmingly loud. The high-pitched din against the treetops was a stark contrast to the low-toned plunk of rain on the rippling river surface. Vigo was thankful this storm lacked thunder and lightning. He was sure it would send him into an anxious fury. All other sounds drowned in the downpour. All Vigo could hear was the cacophony of the storm.

By the time the rain died down to a mist, Vigo's nerves were shot. The sun peeked through the waning clouds and Vigo was thankful that Enzo had given back his cloak. Despite the storm having mostly moved on, the sound of the pounding rain still reverberated in his ears. Vibrations heavier than that of rain drew Vigo's attention. Two lads, no older than eighteen, sopping wet, stared him down. They both held a paring knife in hand. The blades were short and fine-tipped. Meant for peeling and cutting vegetables. These kids were in over their heads.

Vigo glanced at Enzo, who gave him a wary look.

The taller of the boys adjusted his stance, planting his feet firmly on the ground. "Please, we just need the food."

"I do, too," Vigo said. They were nervous. Vigo could hear their hearts beating so fast it almost didn't sound like individual beats. His head went fuzzy for a moment. If these kids didn't leave soon, Vigo was afraid it would happen again.

The shorter boy fixed his gaze on Vigo, and his eyes widened. Then he whispered, "He looks a lot like the description, don't you think?"

The other boy nodded and asked, "What are you doing with that kid?"

Enzo spoke up. "We're just passing through on our way to see my uncle."

"Did he tell you to say that?" the taller boy asked.

Enzo was silent, and Vigo wished he could look at him, but he didn't dare take his eyes off the knives the boys were holding. They knew who he was—what he was. It seemed word travelled fast. Enzo couldn't know, though. Vigo didn't want him to know.

"Come with us, kid. We'll get you where you're going." The shorter boy placed his hand on Enzo's shoulder.

"Hurt him, and I'll kill you," Vigo said. They were harsh words he never thought he would say to anyone. *I'll kill you;* he repeated it in his head. When did murder become his first resort? He was so distracted, he didn't realize when the taller boy slipped behind him. The kid held a knife to his throat, blade flat against his neck. The edge rested in the crook of his chin.

"That's a vegetable knife—you know that, right?"

He could feel the kid behind him shrug. "Still a knife," he said.

"Do you really want to bet on a paring knife?" Vigo tried.

He shrugged again. The knife edge taunted Vigo as it moved with the boy's shoulders. "Reward's worth the risk," he said. He pressed the knife a little deeper to Vigo's neck. The thin blade was sharper than he assumed. Like a paper cut, it sliced neatly into Vigo's skin.

"It stings. I'll give you that."

Vigo put the pieces together. Their faces were slimmer than he remembered but faintly familiar. Shabby clothes, the faint smell of smoke, attempted robbery with paring knives... These kids really had nothing left to lose. They already lost it, and Vigo's the one who took it from them by fire and blood. It seemed the biggest mistake of his 'life' continued to have consequences.

"Aren't you that apple farmer? It's shocking to realize one of our own did such vile things," he whispered darkly.

His words were sharper and cut deeper than the knife at his throat. The kid's heartbeat was so loud now. Thump. Thump. Thump. Thump. Thump. Vigo's vision blurred again.

"Just leave us alone," Enzo said.

His voice was like a clearing in a fog dense wood.

"Enzo, I need you to run away now," Vigo said. His voice was detached. Distant even.

"I'm not going anywhere without you."

"Yes, you will."

Enzo ran to Vigo and clung to his cloak. "I don't want to be alone out there!"

"You won't be. Take Millie."

"Promise you'll come back?"

With one hand, Vigo loosened the knot of his cloak until the strings came free. He shrugged the cloak off, and it fell into Enzo's lap. Even paltry sun rays that snuck through the cloud cover burned. "You know I'll be back for both of you. Now go."

Enzo nodded his head before gathering the cloak into a bundle and pressing it to his chest.

"Go."

So, he did. Enzo hurried off, and Vigo didn't bother to watch. He kept his gaze on the men who held him at knifepoint. "Now, let's talk," he said. He winced as his flesh blistered.

"Not really interested in talking," the shorter boy said.

He stalked up to Vigo and gripped his shoulders tight. His weight pressed down on Vigo, making his knees sink into the soft, moist dirt.

Vigo grimaced. Whatever was in his shoulder sent shock waves of pain down his spine.

They're going to kill me, Vigo thought. The realization wouldn't have fazed him if it weren't for the fact that Enzo was waiting for him to come back alive.

Vigo threw his head back. His skull rattled as it collided with the boy's chest behind him. The knife dragged across his throat in a quick, painful slash when the boy stumbled backwards. Vigo grabbed his neck. Blood flowed from the wound like a leaky spigot, drenching his collarbone.

He took a knee to the chest, and his already pounding head slammed to the ground. The taller brother had regained his bearings and pulled Vigo's head up by his hair before bringing the knife back to his throat. He turned the tip inward on Vigo's jugular and pushed it in fast. As soon as Vigo felt the wooden knife handle press flush to his skin and he choked on his own blood, he knew it was all over. He was finally dying. Enzo would be all alone. Guilt washed over him like his own blood flowing down his front in rivulets.

But that was not the end. *Why? How?* To Vigo's surprise and horror, he yet lived as that dark urge to feed threatened to take over. Vigo lunged forward, sinking his fangs into the brother's forearm. He yelled in pain and flailed, but Vigo grabbed onto him, securing his mouth more firmly as he lapped up the blood streaming over his teeth. The sensation was intoxicating. He hadn't had fresh blood in days, never mind that the blood wasn't fatty, gamey, cold, or congealed. No. It was lean, fresh, smooth, and warm.

"Get this thing off me!"

The brother's panicked plea stopped Vigo stiff. *What am I doing?* He asked himself. The shorter brother barreled him over, pinning him in the wet dirt. The impact was an audible *slap!* The other brother dripped blood as he stood over Vigo.

Vigo grabbed his leg and yanked him to the ground. Then he stood, pulled the knife out of his throat, and said, "Now leave."

It took everything he had to come to a wavering stand. His body was sore and tired and scorched with blisters from the sun peeking out from behind the clouds.

The brothers scrambled away, snatching the basket as they left.

"Damnit!" Vigo yelled. He dropped to his knees. The food was gone, and he lacked the strength to go after it. The threat of losing himself again loomed over him. He gritted his teeth as the sun beat down. The storm had passed, and with it the cloud cover. "Enzo!" he called. "Enzo!"

Enzo came running back with Millie jingling the whole way beside him. He stopped short when he saw Vigo writhing on the ground. "What happened?" he asked.

"The cloak, please," Vigo begged.

Enzo fumbled to open the cloak before laying it across Vigo.

Vigo sighed. "They took it all."

"They can't have," Enzo said. "Maybe they dropped some."

Enzo was frantic as he searched, shoes clopping wetly as he ran around. Then there was silence. Vigo looked at Enzo to see him standing still with a sopping, crinkled paper in hand. His eyes were wide, and his heartbeat raced.

"Enzo, what's wrong?"

He lowered the paper. "It was you. This whole time."

Vigo's heart sank with dread. "What are you talking about?"

Enzo turned the paper over for Vigo to see, and what he saw staggered him. It was a ghastly drawing of him. His face was covered in burns, but it was him none the less. The poster's caption read: WANTED: THE VAMPIRE OF CRYSTAL WATER VILLAGE.

Vampire... It was a word seldom used, but it meant 'devouring evil.'

Vigo was stunned with panic. He knew. Enzo knew what he had done and how he lied.

"Tell me I'm wrong!" Enzo yelled.

Vigo looked away. He couldn't stand the sight of the poster or Enzo's expression of betrayal and fear.

"Please." Enzo's voice cracked, and he sniffled. "Please tell me I'm wrong," he begged.

Vigo balled his hands into fists. There was nothing he could do. "I...I can't."

Enzo dropped the paper and took off running.

"Where are you going?"

"Away from you!"

Millie struggled to keep up with Enzo as she followed him. With each step he took, the distance between them increased.

Vigo forced his stiff, aching body to move. To run. Every stride was a shock of sharp pain that rolled up him in waves from the soles of his feet. Enzo was fast, but Vigo's legs were longer.

"Come back!" he shouted. "You'll get yourself lost."

"I just have to follow the river," Enzo argued. "Now leave me alone!"

"No! Getting robbed isn't the only thing you have to worry about out here."

Vigo had finally numbed to the pain. His advance came easier, quicker.

"You killed Mom and the good doctor and destroyed our home."

Enzo's breathing was loud, and his pace slowed. He was tired.

"What's worse out here than you?" he finished.

"You're right," Vigo said.

Enzo stopped, and Vigo stopped chasing him.

"I'm one of the deadliest things out here, but again, I'm not the only thing out here. Wild animals. Big ones, like predators, are every-where."

"So what? I don't see a difference, except animals are natural, and you're not." Enzo took another step, like he was about to run again.

Vigo copied his stance. "Because it's spring. Moms and their babies are out looking for food, and they won't hesitate to tear you apart if they feel threatened."

Silence.

"I promise I won't hurt you."

"Too late," Enzo said. "But I guess you're right. Just don't get close to me. Okay?"

"Okay."

Vigo was relieved that, for now, he had convinced Enzo to stay, but the sound of Millie's bell jingling as she drew nearer echoed, accentuating the chasm between him and Enzo. The distance gave room for Vigo's troubled thoughts to sink in. His shirt was damp with his own blood clinging to him. It was an uncomfortable reminder of the unfortunate encounter that led him to this point. He felt around his sticky neck. The wounds were still present, including the one carved deep into his jugular. He should have been dead. He wasn't, and that scared him more than the fear of turning monstrous again. At least if he could die, people had a chance of defending against him.

Vampire was a gruesome name for a gruesome creature. Vigo thought it fitting.

Blood of the Loyal
Vigo

The next day presented Vigo with a hard decision. They had a week left until Lloydstone and no food. Millie could solve the problem so easily. Blood for Vigo, a hearty meal for Enzo. The leftovers could become jerky. It was a win all around. Except Millie was more like a pet to Enzo than she was a farm animal. Enzo knew the meat he ate came from animals, but they were never animals he was emotionally attached to. The day was sunny, with low wind. It was perfect for a smoking fire to cure jerky. Vigo wanted to tear his hair out. It had to be done.

"Enzo...we need to talk."

Enzo looked up from his book and said nothing.

Vigo glanced at Millie. 'Enzo, all the fish have already made their way down stream and to the lake near Lloydstone, and I'm not confident we're going to catch anything to eat tonight."

"I can wait a day. I'm not hungry anyway." Enzo went back to reading.

"Skipping meals isn't good for you," Vigo said.

"Neither is spending time with you, but here we are."

Vigo sighed. Even if Enzo was telling the truth, Vigo knew he couldn't go much longer without blood. The sun was getting to him. It gave him a crushing headache, and the hunger he kept at bay by biting the inside of cheeks was making him lightheaded. He had to keep it in check or else.

"Enzo, I'm sorry, but I need to eat, and you should, too."

He crossed his arms, still reading. "You don't eat, and I said I'm not hungry."

Vigo took a moment and a calming breath. "You're right. I don't eat food; I drink blood. And I can't go on like this." Vigo unscrewed the cap of his flask. He tipped it over. Not even a drop dribbled out.

Enzo put his book down, and when his eyes traced the overturned bottle, he sat up straighter. It seemed Vigo finally had his attention.

"I need to drink, and you need to eat eventually."

"And?"

"I have a solution, but I'm afraid you won't like it." Vigo couldn't look at Enzo.

"What is it?" There was an edge in Enzo's voice that told Vigo he was annoyed. He wasn't going to take Vigo's suggestion well.

Vigo gave Enzo an apologetic look before turning his gaze on Millie who innocently munched on some thick, long grass that hung out between her teeth.

"No." Enzo's voice was soft, and after a moment, he said again, "No! You can't be serious."

"Enzo, I'm sorry, but—"

"But nothing!" Enzo left his book on the ground as he jumped up and made his way over to Millie. He hugged her close to his chest.

She was seemingly unbothered and unaware as she continued grinding down the plant matter in her mouth. "You can't take her away, too."

The hateful glare Enzo gave him made Vigo's knees weak. They wobbled, and he wanted to tell Enzo that he had a new plan. He silently wished for another way out. He knew there wasn't one.

"You've had goat before," Vigo tried, and the disgust that crinkled Enzo's face told him it was the wrong thing to say. He sighed. "I understand this is hard, but we don't have another choice."

"I'd rather starve."

"Please," Vigo pleaded. "You know that's not true."

"Why not? I don't have anyone left to care about."

"All right. I'll give you some time to think about it," Vigo said. His nerves were shot, and his head was full of fog. He didn't have the capacity to argue with Enzo, and he really didn't want to.

Vigo left Enzo to mourn Millie's fate as he took up his guitar and began to play. It kept him focused on something other than his guilt and ever-growing hunger. The thought of filling the empty pit in his stomach made his mouth water, and the faintest remembrance of savory blood ghosted on his tongue. Every time his mind wander off, he strummed his strings a little harder. Their stinging vibrations echoed the pain in his shoulder and brought him back. Eventually, it came to a point where it was now or never. Sacrifice Millie or lose himself. He chose the former.

He wasn't sure if it was his trembling, the distant look in his eye, or his pleading that finally made Enzo understand, but he did. He fed Millie a bundle of clovers he had picked and gave her a teary kiss on the cheek and a scratch under the chin before he walked away from what was to come.

With a heavy heart, Vigo approached Millie. He kneeled next to her. She eyed him suspiciously. Vigo knew they weren't each other's favorite, but they tolerated each other over the years, and Vigo liked to believe that tolerance had formed into something akin to unlikely friends whose dysfunction was everyone else's entertainment.

He stroked her neck and patted her on the back. Her hair was stiff and wiry, and she smelled like dirt, but he hated to see her go. He pulled his knife from his pocket. The hilt felt wrong in his hand. It didn't sit quite right, and his grip was off. He was disgusted by the noise his knife made as it sunk into Millie's soft neck. His heart broke from the pained bleat that escaped her muzzle. She staggered, and Vigo held her to him. He supported her as she collapsed into his chest. Her blood soiled his clothes, and Vigo hated how he craved to taste it as it flowed over him. She went quick, but death was never painless.

The rest of the day was spent quietly working over Millie's hide. Vigo sustained burns all over his hands. They blistered, cracked, and oozed. Enzo eyed Vigo.

"I'll be fine. If a knife to the throat didn't kill me, this certainly won't."

Enzo sharpened some green twigs with a rock while Vigo carved out strips of meat with his pocketknife.

"Does it hurt?"

Vigo stopped. "What?"

Enzo continued sharpening the meat skewers. "Does that"—he gestured towards Vigo's hand—"hurt?

"Like holding hot coals in your bare hands," Vigo said.

"Good."

With just that one word, Enzo cut Vigo deeper than any knife.

"I'm sorry," he couldn't help but say.

"I don't care!" Enzo slammed his rock on the ground. "And I don't believe you."

Aside from "do this next" or "this is done," they didn't talk the rest of the day. They barely said anything of substance to each other for the next three.

Millie kept them fed throughout the last of their trip to Lloydstone, and Vigo was thankful for that. Enzo didn't seem to be sleeping any better, but some sleep was better than no sleep. Crossing the border into Lloydstone was simple, navigating the place not so much. The city was much larger than the village they came from. Not to mention the familiar faces around every corner. It seemed like most of the village had fled to Lloydstone instead of somewhere else, like the mining camp directly east of Crystal Water Village.

Vigo kept his head low as he walked the crowded streets in the market district. Sweet cinnamon bread filled the air. Coins clinked as they passed from hand to hand. Wagons and carts pulled by mules and horses rolled down the cobbled stone street without regard for pedestrians. A stand selling square, cotton weave scarves caught Vigo's eye. The cloth ranged from simple, scarcely better looking than bandage wraps, to embroidered silk. The woman behind the stand adorned herself in the fine material, showing it off to an inquiring customer. In one swift motion, Vigo dropped a small palmful of coins on the counter and snatched a plain, black, low-hanging scarf.

"I hope you paid her enough," Enzo remarked bitterly. "After all, haven't you taken too much already?"

Vigo ignored the slight. He tied the scarf around his neck and pulled it up over his nose. He could tread with ease now that hiding his face from bounty hunters just got a lot easier.

Enzo steered clear of the traffic in the road without straying too close to Vigo's side. "What are we doing now?" he asked.

The noise in the street was so loud that if Vigo had worse hearing, he wouldn't have caught Enzo's question. "We're looking for a place to stay, but I don't think we'll find that on this street." Vigo pointed to an intersection. The cross traffic was less than the forward traffic. "We'll turn off up there!"

"Okay!" Enzo yelled above the roaring crowd.

They rounded the intersection, and the off-street was much quieter. Normal-looking houses instead of cluttered shops and pop-up stands lined either side of the road. One building significantly larger than the rest stood out. A hanging sign advertised the place as Bilby's Bar and Inn.

Hardly anyone was inside. There was a bartender behind the bar and a server sweeping up ash next to the fireplace. Three men sat in the corner, talking with full mouths as they scarfed down their food and drink. Vigo sat down at the bar, and Enzo sat in an uneven stool next to him. Enzo rocked back and forth on the stool with his elbows on the counter.

"Careful kid," the bartender said. "You break that, I'll make you fix it."

"That's fine," Enzo said. "I know how to fix a chair."

The bartender gave him a warning look.

Vigo put a hand on Enzo's shoulder. He stopped rocking and shrugged Vigo's hand away.

Vigo was sure Enzo was tired of jerky for breakfast, lunch, afternoon snack, and dinner. "What food are you serving today?" Vigo asked.

The bartender looked both of them up and down. "You two have a northern accent. Is there any chance you're from that town I've been hearing about?"

"That depends. What town are you talking about?"

The bartender smiled. "The one they say was attacked by a flesh-eating demon."

Enzo looked away.

The bartender leaned on the table. "I'm going to be up front with you. If you have the money, I've got food, and I've got a few rooms. If not, then you can get up and leave right now."

Vigo was keenly aware of the remaining coins weighing down his pocket. "How much?" he asked.

The bartender smiled again. "A room for one night only, and two hot meals—"

"One hot meal is fine," Vigo interrupted.

"Okay. For one room and one hot meal, I can do this much." He pulled a note pad, a quill, and an ink jar from under the bar. He mumbled to himself as he dipped the quill in the ink pot and scribbled down some numbers. He slid the pad over to Vigo.

The price was more than Vigo could afford. "What about a single bed room?"

The bartender laughed. "That is the single bed room."

Vigo thought it over again. He didn't have enough for a meal and a room right now, but he wondered if he could double his money tonight when other guests came for a drink. He might be able to gamble his way out of a tight spot or entertain. He was always good at entertaining.

"Put it on a tab," he tried. If he didn't have to pay immediately, he would have little to lose and a lot to gain. "Also, is there a bathing room included in all this?"

"No, the bathing room isn't included. But why would I offer that if I'm not confident you can even pay for the room up front? I can't trust that you're good for a tab."

"What if I pay half now and half tomorrow?"

The bartender tore the front page off his pad and wrote on the page underneath. "Including the double bath rent?" he asked.

"Yes."

"Pay half now and half tomorrow?"

"I promise."

The bartender jabbed the quill at Vigo. "If you don't, you'll be working your tab off."

Vigo dug the coins and a crisp bill out of his pocket. He laid them on the table. "What's for dinner?" he asked.

"Vegetable stew."

Vigo looked at Enzo. "How does that sound?"

Enzo crossed his arms. "It probably won't be as good as Mom's, but I'm sure it'll go down easier than Millie."

"Stew it is!" Vigo said.

The bartender pocketed the money before going to the back room.

It seemed Enzo was still determined to make Vigo pay for his increasing list of crimes against him. It hurt, but Vigo knew he deserved it. He wanted it, in fact. He wanted all of Enzo's ire. He told himself it would keep him focused on his goals to have someone better take care of Enzo, and then somehow find a way to rid the world of his wretched existence. He didn't deserve to live on stolen time.

Damning
Sera

Weeks had passed since Dahlia visited Sera. She saw it as a
bad omen and a sign that maybe she didn't have a chance
of persuading The Council. Sera paced back and forth all over her
cell for weeks. Her nervous feet left a well-worn path of infinite
loops, not unlike the scribbled patterns children leave behind
after dragging sticks through the dirt. Her feet were sore and raw
from the countless steps she gouged into the earth. Her shoes
protected her feet from the iron-rich soil, but all the walking had
worn her skin down. Callouses had already started forming on the
edges of her heels and toes. The pain of walking would have been
unbearable if it wasn't the only thing keeping her sane.

"Sera?" A familiar called to her.

She stopped. It was Dahlia. She came back, hopefully with
news. Hopefully, it was good news.

"Dahlia!" Sera reached for her through the twisted branches of her confines. She wished to hug her close but didn't.

Dahlia squeezed both her hands. She was soft and certainly smelled much nicer than Sera.

"Is he still alive?" Sera asked. Her heart fluttered. If he was dead, she was not ready to hear it.

Dahlia's lips quivered, and Sera knew the news Dahlia bore wasn't good.

"What is it? What happened to him?"

"You should know that someone is coming to escort you to your hearing."

"I don't care about the hearing right now! Is Vigo all right? You checked on him, didn't you?"

Dahlia nodded slowly. "He's alive, but—"

"That's good." Sera breathed out a sigh of relief, and a laugh escaped with it.

"Sera, you should know that—"

A pair of guards approached the cell, and their footsteps cut Dahlia's words.

"We ask that you vacate the premises until further notice," one of them said.

"Vigo's changed," was all Dahlia could say before being ushered away.

Sera hoped to see her again after the hearing.

Sera trembled before The Council. Whether her shaking was from anger or nerves, she wasn't certain, but it was probably a mix of both. She dug her feet into the earth. The pain grounded her in a way that nothing else could at the moment. The only exception was Vigo, if he had been there. Even seeing Dahlia again would have eased her tension.

They weren't here, though, so Sera braved The Council alone again. The throne room was an ancient, hollow oak. The three Council members sat upon twisted oak thrones. Ivy carpeted the ground, snaking over and around the root-born seats, and climbed its way up the walls like curtains or a grand tapestry.

"You're lucky," Elder Lobelia said. She looked down her nose at Sera.

Sera didn't feel lucky. She had been imprisoned for weeks with nothing to do but stew on her fate and fret for Vigo's wellbeing.

"She's right," another elder said. He sat perfectly straight as his hands gripped the edges of the armrests.

Sera clenched her hands into fists, knuckles turning white and fingertips aching in her own grip. She let her anger embolden her. "I disagree greatly," she said. If she didn't face them seemingly undaunted, how else could she demand respect from them? Today was the first in weeks anyone had spoken to her outside of mealtime—aside from Dahlia, of course.

"You broke a law, and like a child, subverted the parent in charge to tattle to the other parent. From what I heard, you might have even thrown a temper tantrum for the Southern Fae Council." The third elder spoke up. She was the youngest of the three, though all of them appeared young. Immortality will do that to you. She lounged in her chair more than she sat. She seemed bored.

Meanwhile, Sera was holding in a hailstorm. She flexed her hands, letting their color return. "I wouldn't call my grievances for attempted murder a temper tantrum." She dug her feet into the soil. Indents formed, and along her heel, a blister popped. The warm liquid oozed all over her ankle, and the tender skin beneath throbbed.

"Of course, you wouldn't think that," the male elder spoke again. "Senseless children never do." Sera didn't think it was possible, but as he raised his voice, his body seemed to rise, too, making him sit straighter and straighter.

Sera took a deep, steadying breath. Now she knew she wasn't trembling in awestruck fear; her rage was seeping out involuntarily. "I love him. And you dusty, flightless, control freaks couldn't just let us be."

The bored elder sat up. "Do you honestly think you're the first fairy to fall in love with a human? I promise you, you aren't. You're not even the first to break our most important rule: never tell a human your true name."

Sera knew that. She and Elder Lobelia shared knowing looks. When Elder Lobelia appeared at her wedding, Sera wasn't sure if her persistence was because of jealousy or true concern; now she was certain it was both and that not even Elder Lobelia herself could untangle the two motives. They were wound together in knots.

Sera hardened her gaze on Elder Lobelia. "Vigo would never do to me what your lover did to you."

She crossed her legs and tilted her head like a predator, ready to pounce. "I sure hope you're right because we have decided to give you what you want."

"What are you talking about?" Sera's heart skipped a beat before plummeting into a dark abyss. She should be elated that she was going to get what she desired most, but the way Elder Lobelia said it didn't fill her with joy but dread.

"By unanimous decision, the Western Fae Council has sentenced you to eternal banishment. I don't know how you did it, but for better or worse, your husband survived my curse. You are powerful but reckless to the point of stupidity. For both your sakes, I hope saving his life is worth it."

Of course, it's worth it. Sera resisted the urge to shout at them. Then she remembered what Dahlia had said. *What did she mean he changed? Changed how?* Those were questions she couldn't wait to answer. She gave the court a bow too quick and shallow to show any real respect, but as far as she was concerned, they were lucky she bowed at all before turning to leave.

Then, the foliage in the room seemed to close in on her. Sera's heart ran away from her, and she was too slow to catch it. Creeping ivy wrapped around her ankles, yanking her to the ground. The vines twisted up her legs with a strangling grip. Her skin swelled red at the edges. A pair of attendants forced her onto her knees.

Elder Lobelia donned a pristine glove. "It seems you forgot to leave behind your wings."

Sera gaped in horror at the implication. Her heart pounded in her chest, seeking freedom. "What?"

"If I let you leave with them, you can still come back, and I specifically told you that you're not allowed to do that."

The doors to the throne room creaked open, and someone bearing a leather-sheathed knife entered the room. They didn't even glance at Sera as they handed the knife to Elder Lobelia. She unsheathed it with an air of superiority. One hand gripped Sera's chin while the other held firmly onto the knife hilt. It had a hot, acrid stench that crinkled her nose. She struggled against the vines as realization set in.

"You know what this is, don't you," Elder Lobelia said.

She nicked Sera's cheek with its sharp edge. The wound burned like she had been struck with a fire poker. It was an iron knife.

Sera had no words. She didn't even know if saying anything would make a difference, and she wasn't going to plead with Lobelia. She gritted her teeth, bracing herself for the dizzying pain.

The blade cut deep, and warm blood dribbled from the growing laceration. She writhed. The vines holding her down squeezed tighter, leaving more than welts and scrapes in their wake. Sera's shrill screams echoed off the hollow space as Lobelia carved up her back. She tugged and hacked until one wing tore free, ripping another scream from Sera's lips. Her vision was blurred by tears that flowed as freely as the blood down her spine.

Lobelia carelessly discarded Sera's right wing. Its bloody, shredded form lay next to her. She reached out with shaking hands. Her fingers grazed its now dull surface. She gasped wetly as her own wing turned to dust beneath her touch. No one spoke as Lobelia continued her onslaught. Sera's left wing met the same fate as her right.

When it was over, Sera was pushed out of the throne room by rough hands gripping her shoulders. Her dress barely clung to her form with all the tears in the bodice. Sera's bleary eyes fell upon Dahlia, who rushed to her side.

"Get back!" the man gripping Sera's shoulders shouted.

Dahlia placed her palm flat on his chest. "Follow us if you must, but I will take her from here." Dahlia's words were firm. A firmness Sera longed for in her willowy state.

He didn't back off.

"I am a member of the Southern Fae Council; you will obey me or face my wrath. I don't make empty threats."

"Let her go," Lobelia said. She rounded them to step in front of Sera. "I will see them off."

The man let Sera go, and Dahlia scooped her up like she weighed nothing. Sera was glad about it, too. She let her head fall to one side against Dahlia's chest as she was carried away.

Dahlia slathered Sera's wounds in a healing balm and wrapped them tight while Lobelia impatiently eyed them from a distance.

"What's wrong with Vigo?" Sera finally asked.

"All I know is that he attacked your village. It's abandoned now."

"And where is he?"

"I don't know. He was with a boy. They were playing guitar last time my butterfly spotted them."

Sera's chest warmed. Vigo couldn't have changed that much. "Are you sure it was him who attacked Crystal Water?"

"Unfortunately."

Sera didn't believe her. Vigo would never do anything like that. He didn't have a reason to. Maybe someone who looked like Vigo had done it.

Sera was promptly marched to the moon gate, where Dahlia embraced her one last time. She slipped something into Sera's pocket. Two somethings. "I love you," she said. Her voice was tear-choked.

"I love you, too."

When they parted, Sera casually put her hands in her pockets. There, her fingers traced the spiraled cut of a Wander Stone and what she assumed was a small jar of salve.

Lobelia activated the gate. Its shifting surface looked the way Sera felt. She was weak in the knees from pain. Her feet. Her back. Even her head throbbed.

"He was headed for Lloydstone. He's probably there now."

Sera stepped through the gate, and from the other side, Lobelia tossed her a forced look of indifference. "Good luck."

Good luck. Those words were like spit in Sera's face.

A Worthy Melody
Vigo

T he patrons at the inn weren't the gambling type, so when Vigo mentioned it to them, they told him about a club where you can find almost anything. He learned that his options were to bet on a fight, get paid to be in one, gamble, or perform.

Alcohol and salty sweat permeated the room. The air was thick and warm, like a bathhouse only less clean. Cheering voices and the sounds of fighting were a steep contrast to the whispered conversations about sex, money, and bets. Vigo squeezed past the multitude of bodies milling about the room. He watched and waited for a couple rounds to pass while dramatic, jaunty music played from another stage across the room. Some of the men waiting for their chance to scrap were burly, broad-shouldered, about 6' tall with the muscles of a laboring man. The smell of fresh blood hung in the air. He gave the flask in his pocket a little shake. It was low. Too low for his liking.

He walked away from the ring and followed the sound of cards and dice to another room. A room of gambling alcoves. He passed by the tables, weighing his options: dice, cards, dominos, marbles, even chess. Marbles was played in the corner, on the floor, of course. Which game did he feel lucky enough to win? None, if he was being honest with himself. Dice was all luck. A good hand in cards relied on it, too. Chess was all strategy, which he could do if he had more practice. While Vigo wasn't a master marbler, he was good, and he found himself drawn to it. It was intimately familiar in a way the other games weren't. He grew up playing marbles with his brother, even until recently. He had taught Enzo how to play. It was his best chance.

He crouched down and asked the people playing to get in on the next match.

The woman running the circle gave him a sideways glance and pointed to a set of numbers drawn in chalk on the wall next to her. "That's the fee," she said.

He was just shy of the sum. "I'll be back," he said.

He left the gambling den with another problem to solve. If he couldn't scrounge up enough change, he just might have to enter the ring. Wanting plan B to be more fleshed out than plan A, he asked around for how to get in a fight. A couple of people he asked had been a little too drunk and told him that they could give him a good fight right there. After that, he went to the bar. He asked the man mixing drinks, hoping to get a more sensible response.

"You take it up with the owner or the fight master, but since you're new, don't expect a big payout. Actually, don't even expect to win," the bartender said.

"I imagine some of them can hit pretty hard," Vigo agreed.

The bartender leaned over the counter. "Ever seen a guy get his jaw socked clean off?"

"Can't say I have," Vigo admitted.

"It can happen. I saw it happen. It was just once, but even if you don't lose a limb in the fight, the injuries you can get aren't easily recovered."

The irony that the thing he hated most about himself was the very same thing that might help him pay the bills wasn't lost on him. "I can take a hit," Vigo said.

Someone shifted next to him.

"Pretty boy like you?" A sultry voice drew his attention.

A woman with dark curls and jewel-colored eyes looked him up and down with a hand on her hip and another around her glass. Her dress had a low-cut lace-up bodice and a slit in the side that showed off her elegantly crossed legs.

"You don't look like the type to wager his life in a place like this. You're too cute to risk a broken nose."

Vigo laughed, but not meanly, at her clear flattery. "Normally, you would be right. I prefer to sing and pick apples."

She set her glass on the table. Her ruby-red smile was sharp. "So, you're desperate for some quick cash?"

"Isn't everyone?"

"Only those with a debt to pay. Is that why you're here? Are you paying a debt to some loan shark?"

"No. No loan shark." *But there is a large debt hanging over my head,* Vigo thought.

"Then you're a farmer with too many kids to feed."

Vigo's lips slipped into a wistful smile. "I was a farmer, but there's only one kid. He's not even mine. I'm just helping him out."

She took another drink. It made him realize that he wanted one to steel his nerves for what was to come. Just because he couldn't die didn't mean getting his ass kicked didn't hurt.

While he wanted a drink, he was well aware that he didn't have the extra coin to spare if he wanted enough money for the gambling fee. Not yet, anyway. Alcohol didn't even taste good anymore, but Vigo wondered if it would still intoxicate him.

He pointed at Cressida's glass. "Is the liquor worth the price?"

"Considering that the owner and I are good business partners, I'm inclined to say yes. But truth be told, I'm working right now, and drinking on the job is against my contract." She raised the glass. "This is tea. My own blend. It helps me look the part of a dark temptress. Is it working?"

Her coy smile was inviting. "It is," Vigo admitted.

Her smile fell. "But not enough."

"I can't even afford a drink. I wouldn't be able to pay you what your services are worth, and I'm short on time."

"Then, let's get you some coin. You said you can't afford a drink, so I assume the gambling den is out of the question, but you also mentioned performing." Her eyes narrowed as she looked him up and down again over the rim of her glass. "What can you do?"

"I can sing and play guitar, but my instrument isn't here with me."

"I can fix that," she said. "We have plenty of loaners lying around."

"I assume at a cost?"

"Don't worry about that. Let's go."

She abandoned her drink and led Vigo away from the bar. Her dark curls bounced as she parted the crowd with just a glance. A path opened for her, like a deer walking a well-worn trail. She was undaunted, graceful, and determined. She walked right up to a portly man whose laugh could be heard above all else. He was chatting with another man who was tall and dark. Dark hair. Dark eyes. Dark attire. His pale skin made for a foreboding contrast against all the black.

"Hello dear," the foreboding man greeted Cressida with a head bow. His voice was smooth and dangerous. "Who's your friend?" he asked.

"Remington," she began. She placed a hand on his shoulder, rubbing her thumb across the edge of his collarbone. "He wants to perform."

The man, apparently named Remington, looked past Cressida with a raised brow. "Do you sing or play?"

"I can do both."

"You'd have to take that scarf off your face to do that," Remington retorted.

The portly man next to him, with a hearty laugh, spoke up. "It could still be entertaining even if he can't sing or play. The crowd hasn't had a good laugh in a while."

"Charles has a point," Cressida argued. "We also have some time before the next fight starts."

Vigo felt Remington's scrutinizing gaze burn a trail as he looked Vigo up and down before turning to Charles. Charles. "It's your club, it's your decision."

Charles shrugged his shoulders. "Why not?" he said.

"I can get you on stage next," Remington offered. "Whether Charles pays you for the performance is another matter entirely, but you can certainly take home any tips."

The near-guaranteed promise of a low sum was unfortunate, but what choice did Vigo have? He needed the money yesterday.

"What about a guitar?" Vigo asked.

"You'll have to get a loan from someone," Charles said. "And fast. You're up next."

"Come with me," Cressida said. She tugged on Vigo's cloak, and he once again followed her through the room like she was his lantern in a dark wood.

They stopped near the stage, where Cressida tapped on a blonde woman's shoulder. She whipped around, squealing before capturing Cressida in a hug. "I was hoping to see you again before you left. Also, I have a client who wants us to work up something special for him tonight. You, me, him, some wax. Maybe a little rope... Oh, and some tea leaves."

"That sounds like an enriching idea, Mable. We can talk more about it later tonight. Right now, though, I need a favor."

Mable eyed Vigo with cheeky suspicion. "Is he involved?"

Cressida cocked her hip and placed a hand on it. "He needs a guitar."

"Oh. Sure."

Vigo wasn't certain how he got his hands on a guitar at no cost, but he wasn't going to complain or pry, even if it looked like it had been left in the rain a couple times. The varnish had been worn away, and the strings were rust-spotted. It was a struggle to tune, and Vigo had to convince himself that it was close enough for a rush.

He stepped onto the stage. It, too, was used and abused with dents and a worn path trailing up the stairs and across the platform. He turned his back to the crowd before pulling his scarf below his chin.

"What's he doing?" someone whispered.

Vigo had never experienced stage fright before, but in that moment, his thoughts went wild, thinking of what-ifs. What if this didn't get him the money he needed? What if someone crept onto the stage to peek at him with his guard down? What if they recognized him as a wanted man?

"Well, are you going to perform, or do I have to take your place?" Cressida called.

The crowd laughed and whooped.

He silenced them with a single chord. It was high-strung and high-sung. Vigo ignored his thoughts as best he could by putting all his energy into the show. As he played, the thunks of coins against wood made his ears twitch with delight. One bounced off his heel, skidding to a stop in another direction. His tense shoulders eased. He sang with more life, more power, more hope.

Desire

Vigo

V igo collected his earnings, counting them as he went. He had a little more than enough for the gambling fee, and that didn't even include what he brought with him. He hurried off the stage and down the steps. Charles bounced up to meet him at the bottom. He offered Vigo his hand to shake. Vigo shifted the guitar from his right to his left and grasped Charles' hand. Charles shook much harder than Vigo expected.

"You were a pleasant surprise this evening," he admitted.

"Thank you."

Charles backed away, and as Vigo descended the last step, a sense of need swept over him. That dark hunger was back. It was small, but it was there. He patted his pockets for his flask. He found it in his front pocket and remembered how empty it was. The sounds of life—laughing, talking, breathing, hearts beating—came together in an overwhelming symphony. He needed to leave before he caused a scene.

"I need some air. Excuse me." He attempted to push past Charles.

Remington stopped him. "I hope to see you again here or even at my place in Port Haddock." He slipped Vigo a card.

Vigo took it without thinking. The crowd, the noise, the scents of liqueur and cigars made him dizzy. He wavered.

"Are you all right?" Charles asked.

"Charles. Remington. Give him some time alone with me. I'll make sure to take care of him."

Charles shuffled off, but Remington stayed.

"Cressida, you're very charming," Vigo said. "And I'm thankful for your help this evening, but I have somewhere to be."

"I'm sure you do, but you can't go anywhere looking like that." She gestured to all of Vigo, who was very aware of how off-kilter he appeared. That's probably because of the way he leaned to one side, using the guitar as a pitiful counterweight to keep him balanced.

Excess saliva pooled in Vigo's mouth, and a lump formed in his throat. He tried looking anywhere but at Cressida. Admittedly, it was difficult not to fixate on the throbbing vein in her gorgeous neck, just above her collarbone. He gave the flask in his pocket another good shake. It was so low. The thought of spending a lust-filled night with Cressida made him feel guilty, but if she let him drink her blood while they did so, he would just add it to the pile of regrets. The safety of those around him was the most important. Especially Enzo.

"Your silence tells me you're not interested. That's all right. Another time, maybe." Her smile showed one thing, while the lilt in her voice revealed another.

"Don't go."

She stopped.

"What are the rules?"

She turned serious. "Follow me somewhere more private."

Vigo left the guitar leaning against the stage and let Cressida lead him back through the thick, noisy crowd and down a hall labeled 'PRIVATE.'

"This is my room." She opened the door and shut it behind them. The room was lit by an oil lamp on a nearby table. Cressida sat on the bed. It was covered over with a pink, sleek sheet that seemed to shimmer.

She crossed one leg over the other and ran a hand over the bed. "Silk is perfect for keeping a steamy night cool. And..." She scrunched a bundle of blankets at the end of the bed. "Wool is fantastic for keeping warm on cooler, calmer evenings."

The phrase 'biting off more than you can chew' came to Vigo's mind.

"I have a rather odd request."

She threw her head back in a genuine laugh. "Excuse me, dear, but there isn't much I haven't done. And There's even less that I'm not willing to try."

Her confidence was reassuring, as was the exchange with Mable he witnessed earlier. "Can I..." Vigo didn't know how to ask this. "How do you feel about biting?"

A smile crossed Cressida's lips. She uncrossed her legs and leaned back on her hands. "Biting is a staple for many. I can give, and I can receive."

Vigo didn't think before he asked, "How hard? Wait—"

Cressida either didn't notice the wait part or didn't care.

"I can bite as hard as you want. As for being on the receiving end, I enjoy being bitten, but I'll be honest, unless I'm really into my partner, I do have a limit. What are you thinking exactly?"

Having to admit aloud what he needed was embarrassing. It was so daunting Vigo had half a mind to apologize profusely before making a very quick and awkward getaway. Then what? He would down the last sip in his flask on the way out the door? That sip wouldn't satiate his hunger; it would probably just make it worse. Vigo thought it akin to eating sweets. Having one bite just won't do. Or, more accurately, a starving man offered a full meal. He won't eat just one bite. His body wouldn't let him.

"How do you feel about blood?"

Cressida raised an eyebrow and leaned forward, resting her chin on her hand, elbow propped on her thigh. "I don't faint at the sight of it or anything of the sort. I cater to mangled men and women nearly nightly."

"No. What I mean is..."

"yes?"

"What if I bit you so hard you bled?"

"So, you have a blood kink?"

Vigo hesitated. He couldn't gauge how she felt about the idea. She'd been so nonchalant about the whole interaction. Meanwhile, Vigo was overthinking, and if it was possible, overheating with embarrassment.

"I guess you could call it that."

"Darker, more carnal sex acts are not beneath me. After all, sometimes the best sex is rough. Sometimes. But I will admit, I didn't assume you were the type."

"And..." Vigo struggled to utter the most important piece of the whole ordeal. "What if I happen to drink your blood?"

"How much are we talking?"

He didn't know.

"Honestly, I'm not entirely sure."

"If I don't know exactly what I'm getting into, I can't agree to anything."

Vigo imagined how it would go. "A cup then."

Cressida was silent. Vigo assumed she was contemplating the idea. Her heart hadn't skipped a beat or significantly changed the whole conversation. If she had any serious concerns, she was good at hiding them.

"If, and I'm saying if here, if I agree to your terms, my terms are that you pay me more than standard."

Vigo patted his pocket of money. If he agreed, he would still have a negative tab at the inn, but he would still have enough to cover the gambling fee, which should fix his debt. If he didn't agree, something much worse was possible. He doffed his cape. "Deal."

Cressida sat up straight and offered her hand to shake. She had soft hands and a firm grip that meant business.

"So," she began. "How do you want to do this?"

That's right. They were about to have sex. For her, the whole thing was just about the sex part. Vigo had been so focused on the blood part he hadn't given a hard thought as to how he was going to do this. He still didn't know what was going on with Sera. But she had been missing for weeks without notice. It was probably safe to assume that whatever they had was over. She hurt him in one of the worst ways possible, but he still missed her.

Even as Cressida beckoned him to her bed with a seductive smile and roaming hands that had his shirt undone in a wink, Vigo hoped Sera had somehow found him. He willed her to walk in on him in bed with another woman. Even if she screamed at him until she was red in the face, he longed to see her again. Seeing her would stop him from doing *this.*

He asked himself why he wanted Sera to be the one straddling him. To be the one stroking him. The one he was about to rely on for his next meal. If he resented her for making him such a loathsome creature, why did he still crave her presence? Her smile, her laugh, her touch? Nothing made sense except the facts. Sera wasn't here, but Cressida was. A woman he barely knew, who barely batted an eye at his sickening request.

She laid down next to him and pulled Vigo to her chest. Her heart rhythm still hadn't changed as she whispered in his ear. "Sweet, I need your participation. I can't do this alone if you want the kink you're looking for."

"Yeah."

"It's all right if you've changed your mind. We can stop here, and you'll owe practically nothing."

"No. I need this."

"That a boy," she whispered. Her warm breath tickled Vigo's neck. "Now, undress me," she said.

Vigo undid her buttons one at a time. The embroidered fabric fell open slowly, revealing the soft skin of her breasts all the way down to her waist. A tingling heat rushed down Vigo's spine and settled in his groin. He slid Cressida's dress below her shoulders and then her breasts. Her heartbeat quickened, and her breathing hitched. She was excited. Even with Cressida half undressed and blushing red with heat, Vigo hesitated to go further.

"Do you prefer being topped?" Cressida asked. "I'm sorry for assuming."

Cressida swapped their places so smoothly, Vigo hadn't even noticed they switched until his pants were gone and he was laid bare for pleasuring. She kissed his neck with teasing teeth that sent excitement coursing through him. He finally went slack in the bed, closed his eyes, and gave in to the sensations of ecstasy.

Every move she made felt calculated or rehearsed. It was nothing like the heat of romantic, passionate need, but it was an enjoyable dance they performed for each other. Nothing like being with Sera, and that's exactly what he needed, so he indulged in the carnal atmosphere. Her full chest was soft and supple in his kneading hands as she playfully rocked her hips back and forth against his.

That dark side that kept him alive wanted more. It always did, and Vigo assumed it always would. He groaned to himself in the form of a faint, frustrated sigh. He hoped Cressida hadn't noticed. Since she was still leaving scorching kisses all over his body, it was safe to think she hadn't.

He sounded out of breath when he said, "I need to bite."

He rolled them over so he was on top again.

Cressida smiled darkly, and her green eyes gleamed in the lamplight. "I've been waiting all night for you to say that," she said. "But I hope you realize that if you're going to bite me, you'll have to take that scarf off."

"Promise you won't tell," he teased. It was a front. Deep down, part of him was terrified of her seeing his face.

"Most of the people who come here have a reputation, not to mention debauchery being our staple. If we went around ratting each other out, we wouldn't have a business worth anyone's time." She looked at him with want in her eyes, and Vigo wanted her, too.

She placed a hand on the back of his head, drawing him close. He let her other hand tear the scarf away and discard it on the floor. "I knew you'd be handsome," she grinned. "Your voice gave it away."

She tilted her head to the side. Ebony curls bounced like a welcome greeting as they fell over her shoulder. Vigo brushed the tresses aside and leaned in for a kiss. He planted a soft one in the crook of her neck. When he grazed his fangs across Cressida's skin, she shivered beneath him. He sank his teeth into her flesh. Her wince morphed into a moan as he sucked. It had been a while since he had tasted fresh blood. He couldn't help the moan that escaped his lips. This was the first time that he didn't loathe what he was. He enjoyed the experience without reservation.

Cressida's blood was warm, slick, and savory. It abated his hunger, filling him with bliss and even more lust. He desired more, but he needed to stop. He promised he would. He pulled away to see the twin marks dotting Cressida's neck smeared with blood. He licked it away as a sensual farewell before kissing her roughly on the lips. She grabbed his shoulders and squeezed. The pain barely registered.

"I want you," she said breathlessly.

And he gave himself to her with ease.

They dressed, and as Vigo paid Cressida what she asked for, she said, "I'm saying this because you have a kid. Try not to involve yourself with Charles and his associates, especially Remington. You seem sweet. I wouldn't want you and that kid to get hurt."

"Thanks, but I don't really have a choice."

"My mother struggled with money when I was young, so I understand. Just be careful."

Vigo donned his scarf again, pulling it up over his nose before he left for the gambling den.

A Biding Affair
Sera

The inn smelled like over-boiled vegetables and wood varnish. A waitress greeted Sera in passing as she twirled around the room, wiping tables and collecting cups.

"Did a tall man with dark hair and a young boy take a room here?" Sera asked.

The waitress didn't even pause as she said, "They did. The man went out, but the boy is upstairs."

"Winny!" a man from the kitchen yelled.

She sighed, rolled her eyes, and hurried back to the kitchen. "What?"

Sera went up the stairs two at a time. When she reached the top, she called out, "Enzo?"

She peered down the hall.

"Enzo?" She called again.

Two doors to her right, a lock clicked. The door swung open wide on whining hinges. In the doorway stood Enzo. Sera's eyes locked with his, and he sprinted toward her. Sera wavered as Enzo barreled into her. His arms flew around her waist, and his hands clutched the fabric of her dress.

"Please take me with you before he gets back."

His knuckles dug into the tender wounds on Sera's back. She winced at the bolts of pain arching between her shoulders.

"Enzo, what's wrong? Where is Vigo?" A dizzying mix of heart-pumping fear and confusion poured over her like a bucket of ice water.

Enzo pulled Sera into his room. Sera shut the door behind them and sat with him on the creaking bed.

"What's going on?" Sera tried again. "Why are you here and not at home?"

"It's gone," Enzo said. He leaned into Sera for another hug, laying his cheek on her shoulder.

Sera wrapped her arms around him, stretching her back muscles, straining the scabbed skin. "I'm sorry, but I don't understand."

"Something's wrong with Vigo. He killed people. He killed my mother. He drinks blood. He destroyed our home. He gets this oozy, blistery rash from the sun. He's a monster, and I don't want anything to do with him," Enzo cried. His tears soaked through the fabric on Sera's shoulder.

Sera couldn't believe what she heard. Vigo, a monster? That didn't sound like the man she fell in love with. Maybe Dahlia hadn't mistaken someone else for Vigo. Either way, she understood next to nothing.

"Hey, look at me," Sera said.

He did. Enzo's face was puffy, and his voice pitchy. "What?"

"You're talking about my husband Vigo, right?"

"Mhm."

Sera thought about how to put it delicately. "How could he have done all that?"

"I don't know, but I don't care. He killed Mom, and I want to go home with you!"

Sera held him close again and rubbed his back. Her head swirled. Lobelia had told her Vigo survived. Told her that somehow Sera had done the impossible and that she hoped it was worth it. At the time, Sera assumed Lobelia was mocking the loss of Sera's wings and her inability to go back to the Fae Realm. Now, she knew she meant that and more because there was something terribly wrong with Vigo.

"It's okay," Sera told Enzo, but it was as much of a reassurance for her as it was for him. "Can you tell me what you're doing here?"

"We were on our way to see my uncle. Vigo said he can take care of me, then... Then I found out that Vigo was the monster who attacked the village."

Hearing Enzo call the man she loved a monster was heartbreaking. She told herself she had no right to be mad or to cry. Now wasn't the time for that because a little boy was grieving. He was grieving loss and betrayal, and Sera knew all too well what that was like. So, she bit back her own cries, blinked her own tears away with magic again, and rocked Enzo with as much care as she could give. He was exhausted. She hoped he would fall asleep so she could wait for Vigo to return. She needed to see him. To talk to him. To hold him. To save him.

Reunion

Vigo

When Vigo opened the door to the rented room at the inn, he expected to see Enzo glaring at him before ignoring him altogether. That was not the scene Vigo walked in on.

Enzo was sleeping peacefully. He wasn't awake because he wasn't alone. Enzo was curled up under a blanket and draped over Sera's lap.

Sera looked at Vigo with a sadness that he instinctively wanted to change. "Hey," she said.

Vigo was stunned. He said nothing back. He just stood in the doorway with a blank stare. He had no words.

"I'm sorry. I—"

"I need a moment."

Vigo turned on his heels and nearly launched himself into the hall. The door shut swiftly behind him. His body was too heavy. His chest was too tight. He propped himself up against the door. Sera was back, and she was right there on the other side of the door. She actually came back for him. Guilt rose up like bile in Vigo's throat. What he did made him sick.

No more than an hour ago, he had indulged in someone else's embrace. He may have needed Cressida's blood, but he didn't have to enjoy her company so much. As he thought it over, he doubted whether he even really needed her blood. He could have gotten that from a butcher shop. There would have been some odd looks tossed his way unless he said he needed it for something like blood soup, but that wasn't anything he couldn't live with. Besides, he hadn't planned to live much longer anyway.

A timid knock on the door sent faint vibrations through Vigo's back. He opened it. Sera stood before him. Behind her, Enzo slept soundly on the bed with a pillow under his head.

"Can we talk?" Sera asked.

"We should," Vigo admitted. "But not here."

They went to the next room. Vigo listened against the door. Silence. It was empty. He opened the door and motioned for Sera to enter first. Vigo followed, shutting the door behind him. He turned to the side, head still downcast and his face obscured by his hood and scarf. He didn't want to look at her. The mere thought of it made him anxious.

"Enzo told me about what happened." Sera tilted her head to the side. "He also told me that you're sick."

"I bet he did." She left him for weeks without a word. Not even a letter. Now she shows up, suddenly concerned.

"He said that the sun causes you a lot of pain. Constant headaches, sunburns that blister and bleed."

"Nasty side effects, aren't they?"

Sera put a hand on Vigo's shoulder. He kept his head down.

"He said you killed people. Including Mia. He wants me to take him to his uncle."

"No." His response was quick, and his gaze shot from the floor to Sera. Her arms were crossed, and her lips were set in a grim line.

"I could have him there in the blink of an eye. Literally."

"I'm not letting him go anywhere with you. You think I trust you with his life after what I got for trusting you with mine?"

Sera's brows knit together. "Fine."

"Why did you come back anyway?" Vigo knew he sounded meaner than he should. If he didn't, he knew he would cry instead.

"Why wouldn't I? I love you."

"That's a little hard to believe when you left me for weeks. I thought I had died until I finally woke up again, and you were nowhere in sight."

"I'm sorry I wasn't there."

"Sorry only does so much. You should have been there when I woke up."

Sera stepped forward with open arms. "I know, but I'm here now."

Vigo backed up. "Here now is too late. I'm not me anymore."

"I didn't think it would take so long." Her voice cracked. She was about to cry.

Vigo avoided looking her in the eye. He could barely handle his own emotions; watching Sera cry would be too much. He looked away again, searching for anything more distracting than her. He settled on a crack in the wall.

"Tell me what happened," Sera said.

"Where did you go?"

Sera bent at her waist as she tried to peer under his hood. "Please look at me. I want to see you."

Her pleas tugged on his heart. He pulled down his hood and slipped the scarf below his chin. "Where did you go?" he asked again.

"I went to see the Elders. I thought you were stuck in limbo. I went to get help and then tried to cut ties with them so we could be happy together without them wanting to meddle anymore. They imprisoned me instead."

Vigo finally, really, looked at her. She had tears in her eyes that shined the same way they did the night he was cursed. It was clear that she loved him now like she loved him then, but that wasn't enough to soften the sharp pains of broken trust. "Would it be cruel for me to say I'm not surprised? They tried to kill me."

"I sought help from a different Council, the Southern Council, but they wouldn't help me. They sent me back to the Western Fae Woods where..."

Something wasn't right. "Where what?"

Sera shrank. Her heart raced in Vigo's ears, and she hugged herself. "Nothing."

Vigo knew she was lying. Something happened, but he wasn't about to pry. He wanted to. He wanted to hold her, sing to her, comfort her, but he needed space. She might have been hurting, but so was he, and it was her fault. Sera came back, but nothing in him had changed. He still didn't want to live just for the sake of living. "I'm not me anymore."

"I know," Sera admitted. There was more she wasn't saying. Vigo could tell by the way she avoided his gaze. It was strange how things flipped so suddenly.

"What did you do to me?" Vigo asked.

"I don't know. I just..." Sera's hands wound themselves in her hair. "I just wanted you to live. I love you so much. I didn't want to lose you. But then..."

"But what?"

"But then I couldn't stop thinking about how pointless it all was." She sank to the floor and folded her arms over her head.

"How pointless what was?" Vigo couldn't stop himself from crouching low to meet her.

Sera trembled. Her shoulders and voice shook. "Saving you."

Vigo rested his arms over his bent knee. His hand twitched. He wanted to hold her, and he didn't.

"If I saved you, it would only be a matter of time before your mortality took you from me. I would be alone to grieve your loss until the world ceased to exist, or at least until I forced myself to stop existing. I couldn't do that. I wouldn't do that. I wanted you and I to spend eternity together farming apples, herding sheep, and throwing solstice parties."

Part of Vigo wanted that, too, because he wanted to be happy again. Being with Sera used to make him happy. Now, he wasn't sure how he felt. Too many thoughts and emotions swirled in his head and heart. It might have been an accident, but she damned him.

"I can't love you right now. I can't even love myself, and I don't want to either."

Sera sniffled, and a tear rolled down her cheek. "Will I ever see you again?"

I don't know." Vigo knew the answer. He couldn't tell her what he was planning. Vigo knew she had the best of intentions. He also knew that if he told her the truth, she would fight for him to stay.

Sera wiped her eyes. "Can I give you a gift?" she asked.

Vigo thought for a moment. "What kind of gift?"

"Something to make your journey easier."

"Easier how?"

Sera pulled herself to stand and looked down on Vigo with emotionless resolve. "As long as you wear the cloak, even if your hand reaches beyond the sleeve, the sun won't burn you. And you won't have headaches, at least not from the sun."

The idea was tempting. Vigo was tired of the headaches and the burns. If it worked, Enzo might be able to have some semblance of a normal sleeping schedule. They could travel during the day and sleep at night. Vigo was about to accept the offer when he realized this whole mess started with magic. Was it wise to tempt fate again?

He stood. "How simple is it?"

"Easy. It's a basic shroud enchantment."

"Is there any way you could mess it up?"

"No."

It would be nice to walk in the sun again without fear or pain. It would be nice to experience that again before he died. But did he deserve that luxury? Maybe he didn't, but Sera was right; it would make the journey easier. *It's a simple spell,* he repeated to himself.

"Okay." Vigo took off his cloak and passed it to her.

She cast her spell, handed the cloak back, and Vigo donned it again. Nothing felt different. Maybe the spell didn't work. The only way to know would be to test it in the morning.

"Thank you," he said.

Sera hesitated. Vigo could hear her heart beating fast, and he saw the unsure look on her face as she stopped herself from reaching out to him.

"Goodbye," she said. She wiped her eyes and forced a smile.

"Bye."

And just like that, Sera left. She was gone. The door closing behind her was like a tolling bell at the end of an hour, the end of day, the end of a year, the end of a life. She was really gone. There was no longer any mystery as to where she was or why she had left. Vigo knew why she left, and where she went after didn't matter because their lives weren't of concern to each other anymore.

In the moment, Vigo was sure that it was the right thing to do. A part of him grieved her absence, though. She had been gone for only a minute, but knowing that was the first minute of forever, Vigo felt like he had wandered from one nightmare and into another. A nightmare he wouldn't wake up from. The only ending to his story was a violent one that was well-deserved and uncomfortably warm.

Longing

Sera

Sera held back tears, even after making it outside. Her eyes welled up like a spring after a rainstorm. She breathed deep and slow, focusing on the cool midnight air filling her lungs. She couldn't cry in the middle of the street. Vigo was just inside, and he would surely hear the screams that so desperately wanted out. Sera longed for home. She held the Wander Stone tight. She pictured her destination and spoke her intent with a trembling voice. Sera closed her eyes, and off she went.

When she opened them again, she found herself standing in the apple orchard. It was cold and silent. Abandoned. Nearly unrecognizable. Sera was home, but it didn't feel like it. She sank to her knees and cried. Her body shook with rage while her eyes shed tears of remorse. In this moment, she was a being of pure, raw emotion. Brimming with unrivaled energy and power. She indulged in all she felt: in all she had become.

Her cries morphed into otherworldly screams. Her wailing echoed across the land, vibrating the ground and shaking the trees. The fresh wounds on her back split open from the force of her release. They wept, too. She had nothing but time left. Memories of what had been, and dreams of what could have happened, had the world not been so imperfect, consumed her. She was a haunting apparition of resignation whose bellowing bid the wind to howl with her.

Eventually, her cries faded as she wandered the orchard. She found her way to a familiar willow firmly rooted next to the meandering stream. She lay next to it and caressed its wispy fronds. She was detached. Teardrops still fell from her cheeks, but the why hardly mattered anymore.

Sera didn't realize when she fell asleep. She only knew that when she woke the next day under the radiant morning sun, she was empty and numb. While she was dead inside, the orchard was alive with bird song. The flowers bloomed with fresh perfume. The sun shone gold on the edges of the trees. Even the long grass in the distance was a sea of shining blades in the new dawn.

Willow fronds tickled Sera's cheeks. She looked up, and a sullen, raspy "oh" escaped her lips. The sound pained her dry throat, which tightened with need, but she couldn't bring herself to do anything about it. She gazed at the sapling and wondered what had possessed her to sleep here of all places. Maybe it was her quiet longing for what could have been that still clawed at her heart from deep within her chest. The feeling came and went often as she lazed beneath the willow by the stream.

It was nearly noon by the time she found the strength to dip her hands in the cool stream, her body and mind still detached from each other. Bright light danced on the surface of the water rushing by. Sera scooped up a mouthful of water and drank deeply. The chill of it quenched her thirst and soothed her throat. She urged herself to see what Vigo had done. What she had done. She didn't feel ready to face it. The stories she had heard were all gruesome tales of an ugly, bloodthirsty creature disfigured by fire and ash. She almost couldn't believe it. Almost.

Then she saw Vigo. He was very different from the man she married. He was sullen and terse. Never mind his abnormal teeth and crimson eyes. It was the darkness in them that unnerved her. Even now, just remembering their dull, eerie appearance was unsettling. *I did that,* she thought.

"I cursed him," she uttered aloud, her mind and body finally one again.

She pushed past the long grass dappled by patches of small wildflowers. Their rough textures hitched on her fingers. It reminded her of her failed attempt in the Southern Fae Forest. Her back twinged with an ache that she knew would always be there. The pain wasn't only skin deep. She felt in her soul the loss of the Fae Realm. A piece of her gone forever. Her wings had been cut with an iron blade. They would never heal, not really. It made her second guess if she had really wanted to never return. It made her question if she really hadn't felt at home there after spending only a few years away.

She laughed, and she cried. They were the silly thoughts of a silly young fairy. She knew now the Fae Realm would always be home, despite not being able to return to it. It was as much home as the orchard was. Neither were particularly hospitable anymore.

Compared to the orchard, the town was a dusty shell that reeked of decay. Sera immediately recognized the sun-bleached leather bag, cracked from weathering the elements. It was the doctor's bag. His body lay nearby. His flesh was discolored by patchy blotches of purple, red, and green. His greyed eyes sat in sunken sockets. The sight and stench turned her stomach.

She found two more bodies in the mass of ash and rubble that used to be the bar. They weren't bodies so much as they were piles of charred bone. She couldn't tell who they were, but she was sure she knew them once. She collected their bones in the skirt of her dress and lay them with the doctor. She searched for others and, thankfully, found none. Three bodies. Enzo had told her that Vigo helped him bury Mia.

Four. Vigo had killed four people. At least four people she knew of. But Sera knew the blame was hers to share. She made Vigo what he was. She was just as responsible. These people deserved proper rights. Mia had gotten hers. It was long overdue for the remaining three to be put to rest as well.

Sera tenderly touched the bones of the deceased. She drew upon what little energy remained in them. There were faint traces of life, of memory. She reached out to them with her being and held them tight. She could lose herself if she wasn't careful. She didn't intend to assimilate the energy but to merely merge temporarily: to find the person within.

She found scorching heat and stifling smoke... and fear. Fear that turned her blood cold. His last moments were spent in torture. Further back, she pushed. That's when she saw him. Vigo's ghastly appearance of blistering flesh and eyes filled with dark intent. She needed to push back further. Go deeper. As much as she wanted to look away, she couldn't. She experienced this man's death at Vigo's hands. Trapped in flames and sooty smog laced with liquor. Her vision dimmed as fire branded her skin, and Vigo's fangs stung like thorns in her neck.

No! She would not lose herself. She forced herself to move deeper. She searched for happier times. Times of laughter and mirth. A party. A wedding. Her wedding. A young woman with berry red hair and azure eyes called her dad.

Henric!

She jumped out. Sera's head pounded. Her vision dizzied before slowing to a standstill. Her eyes flooded with tears that dripped onto the bones in her lap. They were the bartenders' bones. Juniper's father, Henric. She scooted them off her skirt, putting distance between her and Henric. Sera needed a moment. She hugged herself tight, trying to squeeze the image of Vigo from her mind. She had just experienced being murdered by the man she loved.

"That wasn't him," she told herself. "He would never."

But he did. The man he was before she cursed him would never. What or who he was now, would, and did.

Now, she truly understood his contempt for her. But the more she dwelled on what she had seen, what she had felt, what she had learned, compelled her to go back for him. There was no guarantee that he wouldn't hurt Enzo. And the way he said he wasn't sure if they would see each other again was strange. He had been hiding something. He never lied to her before, but white lies to nosy neighbors she had seen and heard him tell. His voice always jumped half an octave when he did so. She had to go back for him. For Enzo's sake, and Vigo's.

He would never let her near, though. So, she grew a lily flower. She picked its petals and molded them into a little white butterfly. She sent it off with a kiss and a breeze.

"Find them," she said. "Watch over them."

The long, dark shadow of shame cast over her. Spying was a dirty act. She forced herself to make peace with it as she tried to convince herself it was necessary. That her spying need only last until Enzo was safe. Then she would let Vigo be for as long as he wished.

Sera delved into the memories of the second person whose remains were nothing but bones. Another death and another life waited for her. After that, she laid them all to rest.

Bargaining
Vigo

Vigo sat at a table in the corner, back to the rest of the room. The inn's dish of the day was blood soup. It was a rich broth of cow blood, beef bone, and vegetable scraps. As a kid, Vigo hated it. Now, it was probably the only normal food he could consume that still tasted fine. He wished he had thought of the meal sooner. If he had, maybe he could have avoided burning his home to the ground. Soft rain pattered on the rooftop. Vigo kept his head down while he ate, hunched over his bowl like a starving dog guarding a meaty morsel. His shoulder eagerly reminded him of the sharp pieces of something embedded there.

Enzo leaned back in his chair. "Where did Sera go?" he asked.

Vigo knew the question was coming, but he still didn't have an answer that wasn't a lie. "She…"

"Where was she anyway? And how did she find us? It's not like you two had been sending letters back and forth."

Vigo took a deep breath. "Enzo."

"Or maybe you were, but you didn't tell me. It wouldn't be the first time you lied or kept a secret from me." Enzo glared at Vigo over his steaming spoon.

A lump formed in Vigo's throat. "I don't have a good answer for you. Can you accept that, at least for now?"

Enzo slammed his front chair legs to the ground and scooted forward. "When is she coming back?"

He swallowed. "It's complicated. I would rather not talk about it right now."

Vigo knew Enzo was expecting Sera to finish the journey with him. He needed to tell him that wasn't going to happen, but how?

The door to the inn creaked open.

"What can I do for you?" The waitress asked.

"I'm just looking for someone," A familiar voice said.

Vigo locked eyes with Cressida, but she wasn't the one the waitress spoke to. Remington seemed to stalk his way up to Vigo. Cressida sauntered up and leaned against the table. Remington sat in the open chair next to Vigo. He didn't waste time with small talk or even a greeting.

"I'm heading back to my club in Port Haddock tomorrow morning. I wouldn't be against you joining me on my trip."

Cressida tapped Vigo on the shoulder. She was smiling, but her eyes weren't. Vigo barely caught the slight head shake she gave. Meanwhile, Enzo quietly spooned another mouthful of soup. Just like his soup, he was simmering.

Vigo looked at Remington again. His legs and arms were crossed.

"That's a generous offer, but I'm leaving tonight," Vigo said.

Remington laughed. "That's not very generous, but this is. How about you wait until tomorrow morning? I'll pay off your tab at the inn, and you travel with me. I have horses, so I'll even be cutting your travel time."

The sooner Vigo got Enzo to his uncle, the better.

"What about food?" Vigo asked.

Remington shrugged. "Food is a given. What kind of host would I be if I didn't keep my guests fed?"

Enzo remained silent. There weren't any vegetables left in his soup. The bowl appeared to be nothing but broth.

"What do you get out of this deal?" Vigo asked.

Remington uncrossed himself. "The promise that once we get to Port Haddock, you'll work for me."

"You have performers." Vigo reminded him.

"But not like you. You're charming, handsome, mysterious. You could do more for me than just musical performances."

Cressida put a hand on Vigo's good shoulder and squeezed. It was a warning.

"I'm sorry, but—"

"I see you as an investment," Remington cut Vigo off. "You're versatile, and I have plenty of jobs you could do for me."

"That's it? You pay for my tab, my travel expenses, cut a quarter off the time, and all I have to do is promise to put out any way you want?"

Remington extended a hand. "Simple as that. And I won't put you in any fights, of course. Don't want to damage that pretty face of yours."

Cressida squeezed tighter, but Vigo didn't care. Remington was making a deal Vigo could only benefit from. It was a shorter journey where Enzo was guaranteed a nice meal every day and not just jerky and nuts.

"Okay." Vigo shook hands with Remington. His cuffs were wet, probably from the rain. "We have a deal."

Vigo didn't intend to uphold his end of the bargain. He didn't have to. He was going to kill himself, after all. Nothing mattered except getting Enzo to his uncle.

Remington left with Cressida. She didn't miss the chance to give Vigo a disappointed glance on her way out the door before opening her umbrella.

"That was a stupid deal," Enzo said. "I'm not going with you." Enzo tipped the bowl up to his lips and drank.

"We've been over this. You can't get to Port Haddock on your own."

Enzo lowered the bowl. "I won't be alone. I'm waiting for Sera to come back."

Vigo sighed. "Sera isn't coming back."

"Yes, she is." Enzo put the bowl back on the table with more force than was necessary. "She promised she would take me."

"Sera makes a lot of promises she can't keep. I told her to leave. She's not coming back."

"You what?" Enzo stood up fast, sending his chair screeching across the floor.

They garnered looks.

"I don't trust Sera anymore."

"You don't trust her, but you expect me to trust you?"

Enzo was right, but it hurt.

"It's difficult for me to explain," Vigo said.

"I don't believe you. I think it's simple." Enzo left. He slammed the door behind him on his way outside and into the rain.

Vigo leapt out of his chair to follow Enzo into the alley. "Wait!"

Enzo stopped. "Why are you even trying anymore? Is it the guilt?"

Vigo froze. The rain pouring down chilled him to the bone, or maybe it was Enzo's icy tone that did it. He didn't know what to say. There was so much that needed to be said, and none of it was easy to explain.

Enzo turned around. He looked Vigo in the eye. "Why did you do it?"

"Do what?" Vigo wasn't sure what Enzo was referring to. He had done so much.

"Why did you destroy what we had back home?"

Vigo wasn't sure because of the rain, but it looked like Enzo was crying.

"I—I didn't mean to. I told you I'm not myself anymore."

"Oh, I know," Enzo said. His cold tone was back. "The sun hurts. You drink blood. Is that what you did to my mom?"

Vigo couldn't bring himself to admit it aloud. He nodded his head. "It was an accident. I didn't... I didn't know how to control it."

"Why couldn't you just let me leave with Sera? You said you can't trust her, but you're the monster who can't control yourself."

Vigo was crying now. His voice was rough and unsteady. Part of him still loved Sera. Maybe he always would. Maybe that's why he was still wearing his wedding band. That part of him was small, but its voice was loud. It was screaming for him to keep her secret. Sera wasn't here, though. She hadn't been there for him in what felt like a lifetime ago. Vigo had lost everyone, and yet Enzo was still standing there. Despite everything, he was giving Vigo another chance. Even though Vigo planned to kill himself, until then, he couldn't stand the thought of letting that chance slip by.

"I think I figured out how to control it." Vigo held up the flask he pulled from his pocket. Blood sloshed around inside.

"Is that what I think it is?"

"Depends, what do you think it is?"

"It was filled with Millie's blood."

"It's just blood soup now," Vigo admitted. "But blood all the same."

Enzo shivered. The rain had soaked him through.

"Can we go back inside and talk?"

"Do you promise to tell me everything?"

That loud voice protested again. "Of course."

Together, they went back inside and dripped water all the way up to their room. The look on the owner's face said that was going to cost extra. Vigo didn't feel bad. Remington had the money.

Enzo wrapped himself in a blanket and sat on the bed. Vigo draped his cloak on the door handle to dry. He remained standing and gave Enzo space.

"Do you remember the last time you saw Sera? The day we picked apples, and I got sick?"

"Yes."

Vigo rubbed his temples. Did Enzo really need to know what Sera was? Couldn't he just leave that part out? He knew he couldn't. He promised to tell Enzo everything, so he did. He told Enzo about the law he and Sera broke by falling in love and getting married. He told him how he was dying because of a curse and that, for better or worse, Sera saved his life with another one. She turned him into the thing he was now, and for that, he couldn't forgive her, let alone trust her not to accidentally hurt Enzo, no matter how well-intentioned she was.

Vigo had Enzo's rapt attention the whole time. He didn't say a word until Vigo had finished his story. Even then, when it was all over, all Enzo had to say was, "I need space."

Vigo made his way downstairs, giving Enzo the space he asked for, and sat at a table. He hadn't forgotten the wooden figure in his pocket. He took it out. It was rough and unshapely, aside from vague curves and what looked like a pair of long ears atop its head. Jacob must have been carving a rabbit. Vigo smiled. They were Jacob's favorite.

Progress
Vigo

The next day, they set out with Remington's caravan, and a little white butterfly seemed to follow them out of town. Enzo said little to Vigo for several days. He would talk to Cressida, but no one else. He read his book and steered clear of the horses unless it was time to ride again. Even then, it took Cressida and Vigo to convince him that he would be fine. He only let Cressida help him into the saddle, and they rode together. The rides were long, and one couldn't read from the back of a horse. Not easily at least.

Enzo opened up, eventually. It was slow, and steady, and it warmed Vigo's heart to hear Enzo say, "Good night," and "Good morning."

Vigo always made sure Enzo ate his fill, and one evening Enzo looked at him with gentle eyes. His voice was soft and low when he asked, "Did you?" It wasn't a slight or edged with malice. Enzo seemed genuinely concerned for Vigo. Whether that concern stemmed from

Vigo's well-being, or from Enzo's fear for his own life, Vigo wasn't sure. He hoped it was the former instead of the latter.

As they drew nearer to the coast, the air thickened. After a particularly muggy ride, they stopped for the night. The fire crackled and popped. It emitted a warm glow that caught Cressida's green eyes just right, making them shine like emeralds in the sun. Enzo read by the fire's glow, and Vigo couldn't help but tell him how bad that was for his eyes.

"But I can't sleep," Enzo said.

Even after traveling by day for almost a week, Enzo still struggled to sleep at night.

"Put it away, please," Vigo insisted.

Enzo placed the book on the ground, the pages flittering in the soft breeze. They settled on a section of the book with missing pages. The lost pages had left behind a fringe still clinging to the binding.

Cressida gave Vigo a questioning look, but he didn't know any more than she had.

"Why are there pages missing?"

"This was Dad's favorite book, and I guess Mom's, too. She gave the book to me like this. She said I wasn't old enough to read some of it. Some people die pretty horribly, so she took them out."

Vigo's heart sank, and he couldn't stop himself from giving Enzo a pitying look, for he had seen his own mother bloody and lifeless. The thought left a bad taste in Vigo's mouth. He never saw his father's body when he died. His mother forbade Enzo to see his father so mangled. He had been ploughing the field when his horse trod on a snake and was bitten. The horse bucked, and Enzo's father ended up under hoof and plough.

Enzo shrugged his shoulders, seemingly unaware of the irony, but Vigo was certain that if he didn't realize it now, he would eventually. He closed the book and tucked it in his pants pocket.

Enzo watched the fire intently. Vigo sensed something unspoken on Enzo's tongue.

"What are you thinking?" He asked.

It was then he realized that Enzo wasn't eyeing the fire, but something shortly past it. Vigo followed his gaze to the warm shine of wood. Enzo was eyeing Vigo's guitar as it peeked out of his tent.

"Go get it," Vigo said.

"Huh?"

Vigo gestured with a nod in the guitar's direction. "Go get it."

This time, Enzo really did look into the fire as he asked, "Are you sure?"

"Of course."

Enzo got up, walked away, and returned with Vigo's guitar in hand and a faint smile on his face. A smile that he very obviously tried to hide. He sat down, legs crossed as he held the guitar awkwardly. Then, he adjusted himself. He still looked stiff, but he held the fretboard steady and strummed. He played with the strings like he had when Vigo first let him play one at a time in ascending and descending order. Then he played something different. Slow and unsure, he plucked the strings in a pattern that didn't sound quite right. Enzo's brows knit together in frustrated concentration.

It brought a smile to Vigo's face as he realized what Enzo attempted. "You need a different chord," Vigo said. He pointed to the fret board. "Place your fingers there."

Enzo's forehead softened as he swapped one chord for another, and he played the tune Vigo taught him. He strummed the pattern over and over again. He even varied the speed at which he played the melody. His face was lit up by a smile and the blazing fire.

"Do you want me to teach you another one?"

Enzo stopped playing. "Could you teach me a whole song?"

Vigo smiled. "Do you remember the string names?"

"Uhh..." He pointed to the top one. "That's E. I think."

"What about the others?"

Enzo handed Vigo the guitar. "Sorry. I don't remember."

Vigo took the guitar. It felt right to hold, and he named the strings and the frets aloud. He demonstrated different chords. Enzo's attention was rapt, but Vigo could tell he was wavering. Enzo swayed, and his eyes blinked more than usual. Vigo played a new tune for Enzo. It was soft and slow, and he realized too late that it was a piece of the song he had performed on his wedding day. He was still thinking about her, and it made him wonder what she was thinking about him. If she was thinking about him at all.

He couldn't stop himself from playing. He couldn't stop himself from sinking into melancholy as the fire danced with a vision. Making love in the night amongst the wilderness of the perfumed orchard. A white butterfly fluttered by, and only when the waking dream faded did Vigo realize the butterfly was real. It flew to him, landing on his guitar, and the scent of lilies carried on the gust of the butterfly's wings kissed his cheeks. Vigo's heart swelled with longing and resentment. Was she watching them?

The thought rushed away from him when pain shot through Vigo's shoulder. Enzo's head had thumped against him. His mouth hung open ever so slightly. Vigo closed it for him. He hadn't even realized how close Enzo had scooted next to him. He doubted if even Enzo knew, so he put his guitar aside and lay Enzo down to rest off of his aching shoulder. He supported Enzo's head and neck with a blanket roll. His breathing was soft and smooth as he slept. Enzo was the most content Vigo had seen him in a long time. He was finally sleeping at night again, and almost a day too late. Tomorrow, they would make it to Port Haddock by evening. A day or two after that, Enzo would be with his uncle, and by noon the next day, Vigo planned to be a burnt husk for the earth to absorb.

But right now, he enjoyed existing. The thought caught him off guard and left him feeling uncertain. When had he started to relax? Vigo assumed that it was a combination of a sudden lack of worry for Enzo's safety, as well as the fact that, for once, they had time to slow down. Vigo wasn't trying to beat some imaginary, ticking clock anymore. He felt in control. Or at least, he was more in control than he had been when he murdered Jacob and during his killing spree. The stable supply of blood from freshly hunted small animals every day probably had something to do with that.

"Are you all right?" Cressida asked.

Vigo took his eyes off the fire, but an imprint stamped itself onto anything he looked at. "Yeah," he said.

Cressida sat, braiding her dark hair. Vigo came to know that she usually did that before bed. "Are you starting to regret the deal you made with Remington?"

"No." Vigo's response was immediate. He hadn't regretted it. In fact, he almost forgot about the deal because upholding the terms didn't matter to him.

"You will." Cressida tied off her first braid with a dull strip of cloth so plain it wouldn't even have been called a ribbon. It looked more akin to bandage material. Just a linen or cotton strip.

"I appreciate your concern, but I have it handled."

Cressida separated the last half of her hair into three equal parts and gestured at Enzo with her eyes. "For his sake, I hope you do."

"Why did you get involved with him, then?" Vigo wondered aloud.

Cressida continued braiding her hair. "People like me have few choices in life."

"What are you talking about?"

"My mother was a witch. I'm not. But having a reputation like that is hard to shake. Makes it hard to find a job."

Vigo vaguely remembered a near-offhand comment Cressida made the night they met. Something about how she saw her mother struggle to take care of her. "Let me guess," Vigo started. "Remington and Charles were the only ones to give you a chance?"

Cressida smiled sadly. "Not exactly." She tied off her second braid with another strip of plain cloth. Then she tossed both braids behind her shoulders. She leaned into the glowing heat of the fire. Her eyes focused on something in the dancing flames. Something even Vigo couldn't see.

"The night we had sex, you seemed taken aback with how unperturbed I was about your blood kink."

Vigo suddenly felt the embarrassing urge to laugh. He didn't. "What about it?" He asked.

"I found out the hard way that many people have a rather 'funny' obsession with witches. The authorities and general public make witches out to be some dangerous mystery full of unbridled unpredictability. A lot more people seek out a thrill like that than they would even admit on a deathbed."

Vigo wasn't sure he quite understood, and something about his face must have made that clear.

"Something about packaging that fear of being magically unpredictable into sex suddenly made me desirable."

"So, Charles and Remington hired you?"

She laughed. "No. Like I said, I'm a business partner. I came to Charles with the idea. He himself being attracted to me in the way that garnered me a lot of money meant an easy yes. I met Remington later."

"Did you make a deal with him, too?"

Cressida stopped staring into the fire. She looked into Vigo's eyes instead. "I did."

Vigo came to realize that kind of eye contact made anyone nervous. Not her. Cressida's heart was as steady and quiet as Enzo's, and he was sound asleep.

"I promised to do something I never thought I would. Just like you, I promised to work *for* Remington. I'm not really a business partner anymore. I'm just another one of his employees."

Cressida glanced around camp at the tents. Remington traveled with two bodyguards, who were frequent fighters at his club.

A cool breeze stirred Enzo, and Vigo covered him over with his cloak. *I can get it back before sunrise,* he thought.

"What did you get out of the deal?"

"Same as you, I suppose. I wanted out of Lloydstone. Too many people knew me there. They knew my mother, too, and not fondly. Working for Remington at his club in Port Haddock gets me exactly that. A new start without the reputation of a witch. At least for a little while anyway."

"Do you regret making a deal with him?"

Cressida sighed. "I'm not sure yet."

"You seemed to at least dislike him when he approached me with an offer."

"I can't say that I truly dislike him. I just didn't want you getting yourself into any trouble."

"Why wouldn't you dislike someone who takes advantage of others?"

"Because everyone is out for themselves. If I had the ability, I'd probably make sure I always came out on top, too. Self-preservation above all else leads to self-actualization, or so my mother told me when she stopped trying to be my mother and dropped me off on some poor farmer's doorstep. Honestly, I'm probably more jealous of Remington than anything."

Vigo supposed he understood. Especially the deep-seated need for preservation. He had agreed to let Sera perform a dark ritual to save his life. Even now, he couldn't forget what they had together. He was keenly aware of the wedding band on his wrist. It glinted in the firelight, like a tease. He wondered if he had done the right thing by sending her away. He convinced himself he had because there could be no future together if he planned to kill himself. Even if he never went through with it, what sense did it make to trust the one who ruined his life, even if she meant to save it? Despite all of it, he couldn't bring himself to take off his wedding band, let alone discard it somewhere. The worst part was he didn't understand why he couldn't either.

The sky was shades of peachy pink and blueish purple by the time they crept up on Port Haddock the next evening. Enzo sat in front of Vigo on their horse, clutching the saddle pommel. Remington directed his horse to fall back and trot in time with Vigo's.

"I'll let you get settled, but tomorrow night," Remington handed Vigo a note with a neatly written address on one side. "Meet me at my club, and we'll get started. He walked ahead again just as smoothly as he had fallen back.

Cressida peered over her shoulder at Vigo. "I'll see you there," she teased.

The call of coastal birds echoed overhead. Enzo's heart fluttered, and he reached to hold Vigo's hand that gripped the reigns.

"Hey, it's all right," Vigo said. "There's nothing to be worried about. Think of it like an adventure. You're the hero about to explore a new place full of new activity and opportunity." Vigo gave Enzo's hand a comforting squeeze.

To Wait

Sera

Three days of digging. Three days of candle lighting. Three days of goodbyes. In the end, Sera's tears were spent. She had none left to give, for it became too exhausting to continue in such a manner. She returned home and ignored the broken window in the kitchen as she headed upstairs and sat on the bed. Sera curled up under the covers to wait and watch through the tiny eyes of her butterfly. She saw Enzo's occasional ire and trepidation towards Vigo and the sorrow that tugged at the corners of Vigo's eyes when he noticed it. She felt the desperate yearning between Vigo and Cressida when they shared quiet moments long after Enzo had fallen asleep or secluded himself to read the same book again and again. It made her blood run cold, racking her with sorrowful chills.

But a golden glint on Vigo's wrist late at night, catching the evening light caught her eye and filled her chest with a flutter and a spark that kept her core warm, and her hope hanging by a thread so taught it threatened to fray. She imagined the thread slacking with ease as she followed it back to him. Although tempted to frolic along the path the butterfly weaved, or better yet, to wander there in the blink of a twinkling star with a curious fairy stone, she did not. It would have been wrong to approach Vigo again. He had to come back to her on his own. She had to wait for him to decide what they would be, or if there even was a them to come again.

Meeting Halfway
Vigo

Vigo booked a room at an inn near the docks. They had a decent view of the sea and the ships coming and going. Tomorrow, they would wait for Enzo's uncle to come to port, and Enzo could go with him. Hopefully then, his life would settle into some sense of normalcy. Until then, for better or worse, Enzo had Vigo to look after him.

Enzo lounged on the bed, head propped up on a straw-stuffed pillow as he read.

"When was the last time you saw your uncle?" Vigo asked.

Enzo shifted on the bed and hugged one of his knees, book abandoned on the pillow. "Hard to say," he said.

Enzo's heart thumped a little harder. Vigo couldn't recall a single time Mia had mentioned a brother. "If it's been that long, I'm sure he won't recognize you."

"Maybe," Enzo mumbled into his knees.

Vigo could tell Enzo was anxious. He sat at the foot of the bed, leaving a corner of mattress between them. "Be honest."

Enzo's heartbeat quickened.

"Is your uncle a good man?"

"Y—yeah. Of course he is."

Enzo was hiding something, but Vigo wasn't going to push him. Enzo had finally opened up again; Vigo feared pushing him any further would set them back. He sighed. "I wish things had turned out differently."

"Me too."

Vigo rolled the tension out of his shoulders. His breath hitched, and he clutched his bad shoulder when it reminded him it was, in fact, still injured. "I'm sorry," he said.

Enzo finally looked at him, still hugging his knees. Then he looked away, flopped back on the bed, and covered his face with one arm. The other dangled off the mattress.

"Do you remember doing it?"

Vigo froze. "What do you mean?" he asked.

Enzo rolled onto his side, still hiding his face. "Do you remember their deaths? How you did it, or... how it felt?"

These were dark thoughts for a boy to have. Unsettling questions to ponder. How long had he been waiting to ask them? Vigo thought back to the day he told Enzo everything. He suspected the questions started forming back then.

"Most of their deaths I don't remember. I doubt I even really recognized anybody. If I had, I..." Vigo wanted to say that if he had recognized them, he probably wouldn't have killed them in the first place, but that wasn't true.

Enzo sat up. "What?"

"I don't remember what I did to most of them, but I saw remnants of what I had done. Even tasted it on my lips."

Enzo grabbed at the red scarf around his neck, rubbing the fabric between his fingers.

"I'm sorry. I said too much."

"No. Tell me more. You said you don't remember most, but that means you remember some, right?"

Vigo bit his lip. The familiar taste of blood wet his tongue. "I remember one."

"Who was it?"

Vigo hoped Enzo wouldn't be offended by his answer. After all, how dare he not remember how he murdered Mia. "Jacob."

"Oh..."

"He was—" Vigo's voice cracked. "He was the first—"Tears pricked the corners of his eyes, and he pressed his palms into them.

"I shouldn't have asked."

Vigo's shoulders tensed with every inhale and shuddered at every exhale. "I'm so sorry," he muttered to himself. He repeated it like a plea for forgiveness.

"I believe you," Enzo said. His voice was small, almost timid. "When I found out, I didn't believe that you were sorry. Then you told me what happened to you, and I wasn't sure what I believed. But I believe you now."

Vigo laughed. It was a strangled noise, like he had been choked. He remembered how terrified Enzo had been of the monster who destroyed his home. Then he hated Vigo. He probably still did, but did it replace the fear, or did it twine together like a mess of bramble thorns?

"Do I scare you?"

"You're not you anymore, but you are. I don't know if that makes sense."

It didn't answer his question, but it made perfect sense. Vigo had been struggling with the same thought for so long, it drove him mad. Drove him to believe that there was no hope of saving himself from what he had become, something twisted and undeserving of the life he stole from others, despite the guilt that told him that even a part of him was still human.

"It's nice to know someone else thinks that, too. I just wish it wasn't you."

Vigo's attention was drawn to the book on the bed. Its' worn leather binding was a testament to how loved it was. The hand-shaped discolored spots made for an obvious assumption; Enzo would probably like to have a new story to read. The idea made the money in Vigo's pocket feel weightier, as if the coins and notes were heavy with purpose.

"It's going to be a while before we see each other again," Vigo said. In truth, he didn't plan on seeing Enzo ever again. But saying it aloud made it more real. The realization sunk in like an armful of bricks piled on his chest.

Enzo seemed distant as he looked away from Vigo again. This time, he peered out the window. His lower jaw worked.

The bricks doubled in weight. As soon as the two had started to really understand each other, Vigo was going to tear them apart again. It didn't seem fair, and Vigo's resolve wavered like the pile of bricks teetering on his chest. *Is sending Enzo away really what's best for him?* Vigo had been sure before that Enzo and the rest of the world would be better without him in it, but now he wasn't so certain. He had spent weeks contemplating death, and now that he was so close to achieving his goals, he was just as torn about them as he was the nature of himself.

He pushed those thoughts into the dark corners of his mind, letting others reform.

"We should find you a new book to take with you," Vigo finally said.

Enzo's eyes lit up. He smiled, and for the first time in a long time, Enzo hugged Vigo. It was a crushing embrace that felt identical to the one Enzo had given him when he returned with Mia's body. The kind of embrace given when someone is afraid of losing the person in front of them. Maybe Enzo was, and that made Vigo afraid. Afraid of sending Enzo off with someone he hardly knew.

The Way Forward
Vigo

V igo and Enzo sat shoulder to shoulder on the dock. It was damp and gritty with seawater. Enzo rolled a clump of salt between his fingers. The lump crumbled onto his pants, leaving white flecks resembling sand on his knees. There was sand, too. It was stuck in the cracks of splitting boards. The dock needed replacing soon, or so Vigo thought. He pulled out his flask, unscrewed the metal lid, and sipped on his tepid beverage. It was full of blood from the market. Vigo paid a high price for it, considering Port Haddock was a fishing community, not a farming one.

A familiar white butterfly hovered nearby. It had perched outside on the windowsill of their inn. It had followed them to the bookstore and even to the dock. Vigo remembered how it smelled like lilies. Like Sera. Now, he was certain she had been keeping an eye on them. The polarizing duo of longing and resentment filled him to the brim, neither giving up space for the other.

"That was a bad lie," Enzo said.

"What?" Enzo's remark caught Vigo off guard and shook him from the thoughts and feelings that threatened to send him down a dark maze of his own creation.

"Your drink." Enzo gestured to Vigo's flask. "You told me it was wine. That was a bad lie."

"Yeah...I know." Vigo stared out into the distance. The waves shimmered in the setting sun. The roiling sea crashed onto the shore, sending salty spray into the sun rays and splashes of rainbow sparkled in the air.

"Thanks again for the book," Enzo said.

"Of course."

Enzo tapped his fingers on the dock as he eyed the guitar slung over Vigo's back. "Can you teach me some more?"

On the horizon, a boat bobbed in the waves. Enzo's heartbeat quickened at the sight.

Vigo swung the guitar around from his back to his front. "We might not have the time for that. Would you like to take this with you instead?"

A silence passed between them. It was drowned out by the waves breaking on the stony shore. Salt water sprayed up onto the deck and at Vigo's face. He crinkled his nose at the pungent, earthy scent of sandy seaweed and fish.

"Better question," Enzo started. "What do you think makes a good parent?"

That wasn't the response Vigo expected, and he couldn't tell where Enzo was going with it, but he answered him anyway. "A good parent is an adult who's always there to make sure you sleep well, eat your fill, live happy, and live longer than they do."

"Sounds like you," Enzo said.

"It's not. You sleep like shit, usually, and I can barely feed myself, let alone you."

"But you don't eat 'real' food."

"That's exactly my point. That's why I'm here on the dock, cringing through the sun rays bouncing off the bay. We're waiting for your uncle to take care of you. Fishing sailors like him make plenty. You can go with him and have the adventure of a lifetime playing with dolphins or whales while your uncle works. And I'll give you this." Vigo held the guitar up and tilted his head. A gesture meant to lighten the mood. The sour way Enzo's lips pursed told him it didn't work.

"I don't even know him."

Vigo shrugged. "He's better than nothing."

"But you're better than him."

I guess that answers my question, Vigo thought. He took another sip from his flask. The coppery smell of blood mixed with the seaside medley was a distasteful combination. "Trust me, I'm not."

"Then leave." Enzo scratched at the salt-crusted over the dock. A board splintered, and Enzo chucked it into the bay.

"Nah," Vigo said. He screwed the lid back on his flask. "I'll wait with you. I want to meet him."

"Why does it matter?" Enzo slammed his fist against the dock. He flinched, and Vigo could tell it hurt. "Either way, you're leaving me with him."

Vigo felt the same. Angry. Angry at how his actions changed his life so drastically. Angry about what he had done. Angry that leaving Enzo with his uncle was tearing them both apart, but greater than his anger was his sorrow. "I understand you're upset, but hitting things isn't the answer."

"It made me feel better."

Vigo tucked his flask away and doffed his guitar. "Let me see your hand."

Enzo held it out but refused to look at Vigo. "It's fine."

Vigo sighed. "I want to make sure he isn't a piece of shit before I commit to this plan. Not that I'm much better," he mumbled to himself.

Enzo went back to scratching at the sea-worn dock. "What would you do if he was?"

"What?"

"What would you do if he was a piece of shit?"

Vigo shifted. He propped his arm on his bent knee. "Probably push him off the pier and hope something bad happens to him."

Enzo stopped playing with the grime. He furrowed his brows as his eyes locked with Vigo's. "So, you'd kill him?"

"I'd kill anybody who hurt you," Vigo remembered how he had hurt Enzo. "It might take me longer than either of us would like, but it'll get done eventually."

"Hypothetically, if my uncle turned out to be a shitty person and you pushed him off the pier, what would happen to me?"

"I hear rich people who can't have kids take in orphans all the time."

"I think I would rather take my chances with the Fae than be a spoiled child."

As the boat approached the docks, the crew shouted and whooped. Some sailors whistled, and Vigo had been so absorbed in himself and Enzo's fate to notice the other people who milled about the deck.

"Sera grew up with the Fae orphans; their lives aren't all that great. Besides, fancy house, fancy food, fancy pets... Spoiled rich kid doesn't sound too bad to me."

"I assume the fairies would be fun, at least."

Vigo snorted. "Depends on who you ask."

Enzo stood. "Then take me to them."

"What?"

"Take me to see the fairies and leave me. They'll think I've been abandoned and take me in." He paused. "Hopefully."

"What about your uncle?"

Enzo rolled his eyes. "I don't have one."

"Hang on a min—"

"I lied."

It was Vigo's turn to stand. His knees wobbled. "Please tell me you're joking."

"That would be a lie."

"Why didn't you tell me this sooner?"

"I—" Enzo's eyes shined like the sea as building tears wet their corners. "I was hoping you would change your mind. Maybe think that sending me to live with an estranged uncle wasn't the best thing, and then you would offer to take care of me, but you didn't."

"I'm sorry. I can't."

"And why not?"

"Because you shouldn't trust me with your life. I don't even trust myself. I'm not the man you need me to be."

Enzo wiped his eyes. "You're right." He picked up Vigo's guitar in one hand and tugged on Vigo's shoulder with his other. "You killed people," Enzo whispered into his ear.

"I'm sorry."

"But that was an accident, and you've changed since then. You're not the same guy who was there for me when my father died. But you're close enough."

Vigo sighed. "Enzo, it's because I care so much that I can't take care of you."

"Can't or won't?"

Enzo's question was plain, simple, and heated, but he was right. Vigo had taken care of Enzo for little over a month. It had been a rough month and a half, give or take a week, but he did it. The only real thing stopping Vigo from changing his mind was his determination to kill himself. From the very beginning, Enzo expressed just how much he needed Vigo, and Vigo was too wrapped up in his own emotions to realize that until now.

Vigo pulled Enzo into a hug. Enzo hugged him back, burying his face in Vigo's chest. They held each other tight. He didn't want to let Enzo go. Part of him was glad an estranged uncle never showed up. If one had, he feared he would have made another mistake. He cherished the time spent teaching Enzo guitar. He was happy to see Enzo so excited and awestruck over a bookstore. He liked the idea of eating dinner together every night, even if he couldn't eat anything but blood soup. Until this moment, Vigo hadn't realized when or even how much he enjoyed living again. What he did know is that Enzo made it possible, and it was obvious that Enzo enjoyed living with Vigo, too.

Vigo could always kill himself later if he really wanted to. He had all the time in the world to do that, but Enzo's life was finite, and if Vigo wanted Enzo to have the world, he knew that meant he would have to be part of it.

"I'm sorry," Vigo said. "You're right. You can stay with me."

Enzo lifted his head to look up at him. His eyes overflowed with tears, and the wet spot he left on Vigo's shirt was cold against his chest.

"But do you want me to stay?" Enzo asked. His voice was nasally, like he had a cold, and he sniffed.

"My life wouldn't be worth living without you in it," Vigo said.

A New Start

Sera

D ays passed at dusk and reset at dawn, and like blood into water, they clouded over, turning into weeks. Sera let the orchard grow wild with waiting. By the time she had ventured outside again, late summer had arrived hot and dry. She lay in the waist-high grass, squinting up at the sky, the sun was a bright white ball circled in gold. A golden circlet not unlike the one on her wrist that she kissed with tender lips. The metal was hot, nearly scorching. Her butterfly had perished under the sun's intensity, and Sera saw no reason to send another, for Vigo had settled on his decision.

For the first time in weeks, Sera was warmed by the sun even as a breeze blew by, sending grassy fronds wavering. She relaxed into the earth's comforting embrace, letting the greenery envelope her as she fell into a restful slumber. The first one in far too long.

Tree leaves turned warm shades of honey orange and wine red. Autumn came blazing with color that faded with the falling leaves. The plants went brittle shades of brown, and the early frost took them. Sera awoke to a chilling darkness. She was stiff and painfully cold. The chill clung to her bones as sharply as the ice crystals on her skin. Her body ached with every movement as she rose from her resting place. Musty leaves heavy with frosty dampness fell away like a rotting curtain to reveal a moonless sky of twinkling stars. Her breath, looking like restless spirits in the wind, was a startling contrast to the warm summer day she had fallen asleep to.

The falling snow glittered like stardust, filling Sera with awe. Her sorrows were lessened by the long sleep. The frozen ground crunched underfoot as she walked. She was drawn towards the willow tree. Its whips were strings of diamonds that chimed in the breeze. Sera reached out to hold one in her hand. The fronds were slick and smooth in her grasp, difficult to hang onto. She rubbed her thumb over the glassy surface before letting it slip away from her. The icy whips clanked together like clashing metal. The metallic sound brought a memory to the surface.

Next to the squeaky well pump, she washed silverware in a metal basin of sudsy water. The forks clanked together as she rummaged around the lukewarm water. Vigo came up behind her and kissed her on the cheek. Sera returned the love with her lips on his. Before she knew it, her hand slacked, and the dish rag plopped into the wash basin with a heavy plunk. Cool water splashed on her, making her jump forward into Vigo's chest. He remained steady and placed a hand on her back. His solid touch radiated a warmth that spread from between her shoulder blades and into her core. Vigo's other hand slid past her waist, grazing her hip as he went to snatch the rag from the water and smiled.

"My turn," he whispered.

His breath against her cheek tickled. Her heart fluttered the same way it did when Vigo had offered her his hand and pulled her up onto the stage at the Harvest Festival.

The memory faded, and Sera found herself shivering again.

She trudged through the snow back to the house. It, too, was cold and dark and slick with ice. Wind howled in through the broken kitchen window. Winter had settled in, and the bite in the air hurt less than knowing her honeymoon would have been in just a few weeks. She skated across the floor to sit at the table and peered around the room. She had done this. She let the house fall apart. Why didn't she fix it? How could she have let her grief consume her in such a way? Then she remembered Lobelia. Sera still hated her for what she had done, but she also understood her a little more. She thought that when this all started, maybe Lobelia really had been looking out for her. Maybe the jealousy hadn't set in until later.

Both of their actions helped sow the seeds of this mess, and it was time to lay it to rest. It was time to move on, or at least try to. Vigo had made his decision, and Sera realized he meant it. He would never come back. It was time to find familiar faces more welcoming than those in her memories. As Sera held tight to the Wander Stone, she hoped her friend in the North would not forsake her for her mistakes.

Forgiving Flame
Vigo

The closer they got, the harder it was for Vigo to temper his rising feelings of unease. The familiar river bend brought back that rainy day. The day Enzo found the reward poster left behind by a couple of young men in way over their heads. The day the lies had shattered like the delicate things they were. It left a bitter taste in Vigo's mouth that stained even the happier days they had spent together up until that point. It was suffocating. Vigo's need for air was an illusion, but it felt real all the same. His pace slowed.

"What's wrong?"

Vigo steeled himself against a tree. Its thick, rough bark was grounding in a way that allowed Vigo to pull himself back from drowning in his thoughts. "I'm terrified," Vigo admitted aloud. A chuckle escaped his lips, and they formed a wry smile. He didn't have any right to feel this way. Enzo was the one wronged. Along with Mia and Jacob... The whole town, really.

Enzo watched Vigo patiently.

A year had passed since the day in the harbor where they waited for an uncle who was never going to show. Vigo had thought he was ready. "I think I'm having second thoughts," he said.

Enzo reached out to him, holding his hand. He was warm. "It would be a waste to turn back now. You won't forgive yourself if you do."

He was right.

Vigo's vision spun into blurry swirls. He dug his fingertips into the knotted tree bark and focused on the green hues of lush grass until the world stilled again.

"Let's keep going," he said.

Together, they journeyed back. Back to the crumbling, abandoned town. Back to the overgrown orchard. Back to where it all began, home. There, they found the orchard grown as wild as the Fae lands and as somber as a cemetery, for it was. The house was worse for wear with a broken window and aging wood. Several bricks from the fire pit had gone askew, and some even completely toppled over. It was brimming with plant debris and showed evidence of once being used as a rabbit nest.

Vigo swallowed hard. Bile crept back up his throat again as shame settled heavily on his shoulders. *What kind of grave is this?* Vigo asked in self-disgust. It was a disgraceful one. He knew what he had to do.

Vigo and Enzo visited Mia's grave. Enzo paid his respects again, and the presence of Mia's soul was far more inviting than the last time. Vigo sat with Enzo until the candle blew out. Then, he searched for the shovel and found it covered in vines. The handle was rotting away, black, soft, and covered in moss. It was old before, but after being left in the elements, it was returning to the earth.

Vigo brought the shovel back to the orchard, where he tore away the fire pit bricks. Jacob deserved better than a crumbling token of the past. Shovel by shovel, Vigo raised Jacob's grave to a mound. From the river, he pulled a large stone. Enzo had offered help. Vigo refused. It was his wrong to right. His brother to lay to rest.

His knees creaked, and his knuckles swelled under its weight as he carried it back to place it carefully atop the raised gravesite. With shaking hands, he drew a single candle from his pocket, along with a match and a crude wooden rabbit. Vigo was a poor whittler but had finished the project Jacob started before he died. The piece of wood Jacob left behind had little shape to it other than a stout body with curves. Vigo set up the candle and lit it. He clutched the small rabbit in his hands as he watched the tiny flame glow steady and bright.

"I'm sorry," he said. His voice was barely a whisper. "Can I talk to you, please?"

The flame wavered, and Vigo tensed. Was it the breeze, or was Jacob answering his call? He waited. And waited. Nothing.

Enzo knelt next to Vigo. "Jacob," he said. "Your brother is really sorry. I know he hurt you. He hurt me, too."

Silence.

If Jacob wasn't ready to reconcile, Vigo wasn't going to force him. He put a hand on Enzo's shoulder. "You don't have to do this," he said.

Enzo ignored him. "He's different now. He's not the brother you remember, but he's also not the brother who killed you. Please, come visit. He misses you."

The flame died, and for a moment, Vigo was certain Jacob had just shut the door in his face. Then it blazed to life, hot and bright like the sun. A familiar presence filled the space in front of him, and the scent of pine shavings enveloped the air around it. Vigo's shoulders relaxed. He placed the rabbit figure on the ground between him and his brother.

"I'm a terrible wood carver, but I thought it would be nice to finish it for you," Vigo offered. Then he and Enzo went on telling him about their time together. How they traveled across the country to find a man who didn't even exist, and how traveling along the river at night wasn't even the most difficult part of their trip. They told him of their time spent living by the sea with Cressida. And, of course, Vigo laid bare his warring feelings for Sera.

When he had finished, the wind whipped around him like a cool embrace while the candle remained as fierce as ever, radiating a warmth unlike any other until it burned out.

Epilogue One
Vigo

Vigo's cheek thumped with a bruise, and he was pretty sure the stabbing pain in his side was a broken rib or two. He took a swig from his flask. The swelling on his cheek went down, and the pain subsided. There wasn't enough left in the flask to heal his ribs, though. He stuffed the empty bottle back into his pocket amongst his earnings. The paper notes crinkled stiffly, and the coins tinked against the flask. He played and sang at Remington's that evening. That went fine, aside from the fact that the tips were abysmal. He tried to double his money at a gambling booth. Some guy accused him of cheating when he pulled one too many wins. Vigo took the beating and kept the money. He didn't cheat; he just got good at cards over the years while working for Remington. Something unsettling settled in the air. Part of him regretted coming here tonight, but he didn't have a choice.

The days and hours listed on Vigo's timecard flashed in his mind. In the coming week, he had three days instead of four, which was two less than when he started six years ago. He used to work five days a week at the butcher shop. It was decent pay, and Vigo had access to almost all the blood he needed. There were even occasions when Vigo got to bring home meat on the edge of expiring for free. The job was a win all around. That didn't seem to be the case anymore.

Unlike Vigo, Enzo had plenty of work. Fish were abundant in the bay and its surrounding reefs. It was a cheap meal that didn't need a butcher to process it. Fish could be sold whole and easily prepped at home. When the recession first hit, people didn't mind buying premium meat from the butcher. No one thought the dip in the economy would last long. They were wrong.

It was unfortunate, but Vigo did have to swallow his pride and go back to Remington. The realization subsided Vigo's regret only a little as a cool sea breeze rolling off the coast greeted him outside the club. Enzo would be home from his fishing rotation the next day, and Vigo couldn't wait to see him. The ships sailed out three days at a time, and then the crews would swap. Those coming home worked on the docks for the next three days. The fourth day was a day off, and when the ship came back to port, the cycle began again.

Remington must have followed Vigo into the street because he called after him.

"Long time no see," Remington said. "We need to talk."

"Cressida is expecting me. I can't tonight."

Vigo didn't bother stopping or even paying Remington a glance. He hoped he would just let him go, but he should have known better. Remington's footsteps sped up, and Vigo sighed as he came to a dead stop.

Remington stepped in front of Vigo. "I insist," he said.

"I'm sure you do, but—"

"Here's the thing." Remington put a hand on Vigo's shoulder. He pushed his thumb down on a pressure point.

Vigo refused to give him a pained reaction, despite it being his bad shoulder. Showing Remington fear was like giving him your own knife to torture you with. Stupid.

"Here's the thing. You can't say no. You owe me."

"I don't recall you doing me any favors, but I do remember helping you bring in lots of revenue as one of your entertainers, serenading your customers with charm and talent on and off stage."

Vigo pushed past Remington and started walking again.

"I let you leave. I even let you take one of my other best entertainers with you."

Vigo slowed his pace.

"You and Cressida ghosted me, and I let you live. Then you show up here expecting a cash grab during tough times like you never did anything wrong. I let you come and go as you please. Most aren't so lucky. So, yes. I have indeed given you a favor. I've done a few if you count the fact that I haven't sent authorities after you."

Vigo stopped.

"I finally seem to have your attention."

The brick road beneath Vigo's feet felt less stable all of a sudden, or maybe Remington's persistence was starting to get to him. "What have I done that warrants an arrest?" Vigo put on a false front full of bravado.

"Scraps are inevitable in this line of work no matter your position, and I've seen you involved in some heated disagreements. Tonight, alone, I saw you decked down to the floor, and absolutely wailed on. What you can do isn't natural, you know. My seasoned fighters don't bounce back as well as you do. No one breaks a bone one night and comes back the next like nothing happened. Almost makes me regret not training you to fight instead, but your other talents were much more desirable."

Vigo shrugged. "I'm a fast healer."

"You're so good, in fact, some might say you're magical."

Vigo sighed. "I'm not a witch, Remington."

"You might not be. How's Cressida's tea shop going? I heard no one wants to buy herbal remedies from someone who isn't a physician. Not anymore, at least."

Remington was right. Ever since the crusade against witches started a few months ago, almost no one had been buying from Cressida's tea shop. Her dream had been ruined by bigoted fear-mongering and the recession.

"Cressida isn't a witch," Vigo said.

"I know her mother was."

"That doesn't mean she is."

"If she isn't a witch, then you are, and that means you lied to me. The bruise on your cheek is already gone, after all."

Vigo finally gave Remington his full attention. "What do you want?"

Remington put his hands up and feigned offense. "There's no need to be hostile. I just have a business proposition for you."

Vigo had a vague assumption of what Remington wanted, and if he was right, Remington wasn't going to be happy with his response.

"What's your offer?" Vigo asked.

"I want you to use your magic on the boys in the ring. Even the playing field a little bit. Maybe keep the crowd guessing. It keeps them interested. I'll even let you pick a different recipient every night if you want. And considering the fact that you haven't aged a day since we met, I want to try it out, too."

"I'm sorry, Remington. I can't do that."

Remington sighed. "I'll give you a few days to change your mind. If you don't, you might want to leave town."

"Just so we're clear, are you threatening me?"

"I'm just informing you that word travels fast on the heels of fear, especially when witchcraft is involved."

"I'm not a witch, and neither is Cressida."

"Try convincing the collective of that. Witches have never been well-liked, but we both know a witch accusation right now is like lighting a dry haystack during a drought, uncontrollable and devastating."

"Goodnight, Remington." Vigo started walking again.

"If you do change your mind, tell dear Cressida she's always welcome back. I adore her. She was one of my best, too."

Vigo didn't dare look back. He knew all he would see was an evil specter sneering back at him. Vigo was tense the whole way home. He peered down every alley. He homed in on every footstep that wasn't his own, no matter how close or far. He was certain Remington wasn't going to stop demanding. He also couldn't give in, no matter how threatening or tempting their encounter had been. It was a battle of wills, and Vigo refused to make another him. He wasn't even supposed to still be alive. Not originally, anyway.

He didn't regret living anymore. He didn't even resent Sera anymore for making him. He only regretted her absence and resented the missing weight on his wrist. He had lost his wedding band eight years ago. He didn't even know how it happened. It disappeared one day, and every day since, he refused to let himself forget how careless he must have been to lose something and someone so precious.

When Vigo walked in the door, Cressida was waiting in a plush leather chair with her arms crossed and a scowl on her face. She was obviously less than pleased.

"You look like shit," she said.

"I can see you're too mad to be concerned." Vigo sat on the couch across from her.

"I stopped being concerned years ago."

Cressida got up from her chair and crossed the expanse of their living room. She shoved a ceramic jar into Vigo's chest. "Drink up," she said.

Vigo uncorked the jar with a wet, hollow *pop*. "How did you know?"

"You're never home this late unless you saw Remington."

"I haven't done that in years, though."

"Money's tight, and I know how you think."

Vigo raised his brows, and the jug in agreement before taking a sip. He sat it down in his lap. "I'm sorry," he said.

"You should be."

"No. I mean. I'm really sorry."

Cressida placed a warm, comforting hand on Vigo's thigh. "I understand why you did it," she started. "I'm just mad that you didn't consult me before getting us involved with him again. We were out, and I'm sure he asked for me back."

Vigo nodded his head and took another sip. He shifted uncomfortably. His body was stiff. He guessed he was still on high alert, and Cressida must have noticed.

"There's more to tell, isn't there?"

Vigo gave Cressida a weary glance over the top of his bottle.

"So, what did Remington say?"

He fiddled with the jug and peered through the opening to watch the dark, red liquid inside swirl. "He threatened me. Threatened us."

Cressida grabbed his chin, pulling Vigo to look at her. Her emerald eyes darkened as her brows furrowed. Her mouth was a thin, serious line. "Be specific," she said.

"He thinks I'm a witch. If I don't do what he says, he'll tell."

"You can't be serious. After all we did for him. The town is already weary of me. If he lets it slip that you're a witch, we're dead."

"He knows that."

"Then give him what he wants, and then tell him we're done."

"I can't do that." Vigo put the jar on the ground. It made a dense *thump* against the dark-stained wood floor.

"Why not?"

Vigo avoided Cressida's piercing gaze. Was this going to be how he confessed? After all this time, was he going to have to admit that he was a vampire and not a witch like she thought? Would she still think he wasn't wrong to exist?

"He wants me on his staff."

"For what?"

"He wants me to heal the fighters. He thinks it will make things more interesting. More interesting means more money and more investors."

Cressida's stern expression softened. Her eyebrows relaxed, and her narrowed eyes opened to something akin to fear. "You can't take a permanent position with him."

"I know. That's why we'll leave tomorrow. I'll take a half day at work, and when Enzo gets home, we leave town."

Cressida stood. "What about working something else out? We can't just leave. It'll never work."

Vigo rose from the sofa and wrapped his arms around Cressida. He swayed with her and said, "Yes, we can. You just have to trust me."

Epilogue Two
Vigo

V igo hurried home after his last day of work. His boss made a show of being disappointed that Vigo quit so suddenly. It was an act. With all the problems the business was having, Vigo was sure his boss felt relief more than anything. He had one less worker to schedule or pay.

Vigo came home to a familiar yet unwanted face. It was Remington and a couple of his employees. Employees who beat each other for a living.

Remington held Enzo across his chest with a dagger to his side. One of his employees held Cressida by the hair with a foot on her back, pressing her down on her knees and onto the floor.

"Welcome home," Remington said.

"The welcome isn't very warm," Vigo sneered.

Remington shrugged. "What else do you expect when you leave an old friend out to dry." Vigo shut the door behind him. "We're not friends."

"That was your first mistake."

"What do you want?"

"You know what I want."

Vigo's ears were filled with heartbeats. All beating at different rates and rhythms. "I can't do what you think I can do."

"You misunderstand. I'm not asking anymore."

Vigo finally noticed a sour, acrid smell in the air.

"See this." Remington wiggled the dagger. It glinted wetly.

Enzo flinched.

"This is coated in poison. The poison comes from a very tricky sea creature.

"There is no cure."

"You're bluffing," Vigo challenged.

Enzo's heart sped up.

"Go ahead and ask the kid. He works with fish every day; I'm sure he can tell you all about it."

Enzo took a shallow breath and steadied his gaze on Vigo. "There is a fish commonly caught in the nets off the reef. Deadly poisonous."

"Believe me yet?"

"He doesn't bluff!" Cressida yelled.

A high-pitched *smack* rang out, and Vigo saw Cressida's cheek swell pink and purple.

"Now," Remington said. "Tell me how you do what you do, and the next time we meet, we'll be best friends. Don't, and I can't guarantee that you won't be a family member short," Remington said.

Vigo was silent. He wasn't a witch. He couldn't give them what they wanted.

"Clock's ticking." Remington tightened his grip across Enzo's chest and flexed his hand on the dagger hilt.

Enzo was quiet. He was terribly scared, but if he so much as trembled, the poisoned tip would prick him. He looked at Vigo like a lost puppy. The same watery eyes that stared at him that night twelve years ago. He wasn't grown back then. He was an adult now, but that still seemed so young to Vigo. Enzo deserved a full life. A happy life. He thought he had given that to him. Turns out all Vigo could do was put him in danger. Vigo had finally decided on what to do, but Cressida spoke up first.

"He keeps potions in the cellar."

"Cress!" Enzo exclaimed.

"Go get it," Remington said.

The man holding Cressida down let her hair go and lifted his foot off her back so she could stand. She pulled back the rug, revealing the cellar door.

"Just remember our deal," Cressida spat. Blood painted the corner of her mouth.

Vigo was taken aback. "What do you mean you had a deal?" He asked. He glanced at Enzo who was as pale as a sheet and stiff with fear. Then he looked between Remington and Cressida. "What deal?" He asked again.

Cressida's eyes went downcast before she promptly opened the cellar door. She and Remington's employee descended into the depths.

"She was smart and hedged her bets. Even a suspected witch can't afford to be loyal to anyone but herself," Remington said.

Vigo was shocked. Stunned. That's why Remington was here. Cressida sold Vigo out to save herself. He was surprised, but he shouldn't have been.

Cressida emerged with a ceramic jug.

"There she is," Remington said. "Now, put the jar down."

She did.

"It's not what you think it is." Vigo said. "I—"

Remington yanked Enzo around. "I'm not talking to you right now. Bill, break her nose."

He did. He slugged her so hard, Vigo was sure you didn't need magical hearing to notice the audible '*crack.*' She collapsed on the floor, silent tears running down her face. They mixed with the blood from her nose, sending scarlet trails over her lips before dripping off her chin.

"I apologize, dear. I can't risk anything unnecessary happening to one of my men."

Vigo clenched his fists.

"Don't move, or your son gets it." Remington directed his attention back to Cressida. "Now, if you would, please drink from the jar you so helpfully provided us. If you're telling the truth, you'll be fine. Better, actually."

Cressida breathed through her mouth as she crawled over to the jar. She popped the cork, and her face crinkled. "It smells like death. I can't believe you drink this," she said. Her voice was nasally and strained.

"Just get on with it."

She breathed deeply, held her breath, and took a full drink. As soon as she swallowed the mouthful, it came right back up in heaves. Everything in her stomach emptied onto the floor in a gooey, acrid mess that stung Vigo's nostrils even from across the room.

"Looks like someone lied," Remington remarked.

"I don't"—Cressida gagged out another cough, but nothing else came out—"understand."

"I can explain!" Vigo shouted.

Remington rammed the dagger into Enzo's side. "Then hurry up." Enzo crumpled into a ball, and Vigo raced to catch him. Enzo clutched his side as he fell into Vigo's chest.

"Kid's got ten minutes left. Tops. So, by all means, save his life, but do it fast. I'll be watching closely."

Vigo cradled Enzo in his arms as he lowered both of them to the floor. He laid in Vigo's lap, head resting in the crook of Vigo's elbow.

"I don't want to die." Enzo's voice cracked, and the tears he had been holding back trickled down his cheeks.

Vigo hushed Enzo. "I know, but saving you isn't so simple."

"Just do it!" Cressida yelled.

He ignored her.

"I'm just disappointed that drowning isn't how I go. I hear there's a lovely siren at the bottom of the sea who makes it painless," Enzo said.

Vigo failed to stifle a laugh. "Where'd you hear that?"

Enzo laughed at himself "The sailors have a lot of silly myths. Not sure why I remembered that one, but I'm glad I did because it made you laugh even while I'm dying."

"Tick tok!" Remington pushed.

Remington was rude, but he was right. Vigo sensed Enzo fading. His heartbeat had slowed, and he was pale. He shivered ever so slightly in his arms.

Vigo remembered the night he destroyed the town. He remembered gaining control as a man died in his lap. He remembered the man bit him and how he turned. "If I can save you, you won't be you anymore."

"That's okay."

"No. It's not. You would be a monster just like—"

Remington groaned. "If he dies before you cut to the chase, I'll have to use Cressida next."

"You son of a bitch!" Cressida yelled.

Vigo tuned them all out. "You would be just like me."

Enzo squeezed Vigo's hand. It was weak. "That's not so bad...because we would still have each other."

Vigo glanced at the clock ticking away on the wall. Enzo shivered in his arms. "Are you really prepared for all normal food and drink to taste like mud?"

Enzo nodded his head.

"You've seen what happens if I don't eat in time. Are you prepared to live in fear of that every day?"

Enzo's laugh turned into a cough. "You're the only one still afraid of that."

Vigo took Enzo's arm by the wrist. Alarm bells chimed as he opened his mouth and extended his fangs. What he planned to do to Enzo felt wrong. Vigo had spent the last twelve years keeping Enzo safe, especially from him. All that seemed to have been thrown away in a matter of minutes. Then he wondered if Sera had felt the same when he was dying.

As Vigo latched onto the veins in Enzo's wrist, he couldn't shake the thought that he was condemning Enzo to a life worse than death. He finally felt what it was like to be the one losing someone you cared about so deeply while also having the power to save them. Power that came with a hefty price. The only difference was that he and Enzo knew exactly what would happen if this worked.

He cringed when Enzo's blood flowed between his teeth and over his tongue.

"Do I taste that bad?"

He did. The poison coursing through Enzo made his blood bitter. It had an acidic bite that stung its way down Vigo's throat.

Vigo stopped drinking and wiped his mouth on his sleeve. "I promise you, I'll taste worse," he said. As sinister as the thought sounded at first, part of Vigo hoped Enzo wouldn't have the stomach to choke it down. "I need that jar and some food. Cheese, fruit, bread, anything."

Remington snapped his fingers, and his indistinguishable tag-alongs were swift to respond. Vigo bit into his own wrist, tearing open his skin, and bitter blood flowed. Bitter like medicine, Vigo thought. Or so he hoped. He put the wound against Enzo's mouth. "You have to drink my blood now."

Enzo did. He made displeased faces as he licked the blood dribbling from Vigo's cut.

"I told you it would be gross."

Enzo laughed, choking on the blood. It smeared down his chin, but he smiled.

Vigo lifted Enzo's shirt to see the wound stitching itself back together. Not even a scar remained.

"Did it work?" Enzo asked.

"It worked." Vigo sighed. He couldn't decide if he was disappointed or relieved.

"You don't sound very happy about that."

"Don't worry about it. How do you feel?" Vigo asked. He hoped that by some miracle Enzo had simply been cured without suffering the curse.

"Better."

"Good. I think." Vigo helped Enzo sit up right. He supported him against his chest, and jerked his head at one of Remington's henchmen. "Toss me the apple."

He did, and Vigo caught it effortlessly.

"Here." He offered Enzo the apple.

Enzo bit down and tore out a hunk. Vigo didn't even need to look at the teeth marks on the apple to know they didn't look human. The surprised look on Enzo's face before he spat the half-chewed apple chunk on the floor told him that Vigo had not only healed Enzo, but he had cursed him, too.

"Now I can see why you hate eating," Enzo remarked.

"That's it?" Remington finally spoke. "He's cured?"

Vigo lifted Enzo's shirt again and pointed to the spot Enzo had been stabbed. "Look for yourself."

"Good," Remington deadpanned. "Now make me immortal, and I promise to avoid your pathetic path for as long we live, which I assume is forever. I would be terribly disappointed if that weren't so."

Vigo clenched his fists. Giving the curse to someone like Remington was worse than a bad idea, but he knew it had to be done. He had already threatened Cressida, and as much as Vigo despised her for selling him out, he understood why she did it. She was a bloodied mess of tears. Fear made her whiter than freshly laundered wool. She didn't deserve this. Enzo didn't deserve this.

"Fine."

"Good. Now—"

Vigo cut him off. He couldn't stop himself from tackling Remington to the ground, and latching his fangs in the bastard's neck. Vigo wanted to drain the blood from his body and watch the light in his eyes fade to dark emptiness. He wanted to pulverize his bones into dust and leave his corpse to fertilize the earth. Someone like him was better dead than alive.

Vigo almost did him in, but he stopped himself. He knew that Remington's *friends* would come after him—or worse. Vigo drew back.

Remington sat up straight and fixed his jacket. "You almost killed me."

"But I didn't."

Vigo angrily and regretfully shoved his arm into Remington's mouth. Remington drank Vigo's blood, and the mere idea made Vigo squirm. He tore his arm away.

"That should be enough," he said.

"How do I know it worked?"

"I can help with that," Vigo said. He was sure he had a sinister glint in his eyes. He didn't even try to hide it.

"It would only be fair."

Vigo scoffed. Fair. Remington had an interesting interpretation of fair, but Vigo was happy enough to take the free shot. He broke Remington's fingers. One at a time. Remington groaned and cursed.

"Is all five fucking necessary?!"

"It is for me. Now, where is that jar I asked for?"

Remington waved his men over who promptly set the jar of blood next to him. He drank deeply, and unfortunately, every bone in every finger straightened out, snapped together, and mended.

Remington stretched his fingers out before pulling them into a fist. "Much better," he said.

"Great. Now get out of my house."

"Pleasure," Remington said. As he made his way out the door with his fighters in tow, he added, "Don't worry about the witch scare or any accusations. Your secret's my secret now, and it's safe with me."

He looked back to leave Vigo with a smug smile and a pompous wave before the door shut behind him.

"You should have some, too." Vigo handed Enzo the jar.

He eyed it suspiciously. "Please tell me this tastes good."

"Depends on whether you like cow," Vigo said as he stood up.

He went over to Cressida. She was a bloody, teary mess, but he held her in his arms without hesitation. They rocked back and forth together. "I'll get the doctor and have Enzo draw a bath.

"On it." Enzo got up and took the jug with him.

"Your betrayal hurts," Vigo said. "But it makes me angry more than anything." His fists tightened. "You risked Enzo's life today."

Cressida laughed. It was humorless and cruel sounding. "Enzo was like a son to me, but he wasn't. Even my own mother tossed me aside to better herself. Why wouldn't I do the same with my own life on the line?"

"I thought you cared more than she did."

"I cared more than you did. You never trusted me or loved me enough to share your secrets or your thoughts, just your bed."

Vigo shrunk back from Cressida. His arms no longer held her, comforting her. Why should he?

Vigo rubbed his wrist. The lightness of his hand without the wedding band created a spiked chain that wrapped around his heart. It was then that he accepted the shameful truth he had denied until now. "You're right. I can't love you as much as you want to me to."

Cressida's eyes flicked to Vigo's fidgeting hands, and a scowl crept its way onto her face.

Like a striking snake, she yanked something golden from her pocket and threw it. A shining gold band soared across the room and thumped against the wall before clattering to the ground.

"Take it and leave," Cressida said.

Vigo's heart fluttered as realization set in. He scrambled over to his wedding band and slipped it over his wrist. It was the wedge that loosened the spiked chain piercing his heart, but just like his remorse surrounding Sera and what almost was, the chain would never leave.

"You had it this whole time." It was a statement, not a question.

"I had hoped that with it gone, you would move on and finally choose me."

"I'm sorry." The words left his lips before thinking, and it irritated him more. He didn't want to be sorry.

Cressida sighed and bared her teeth. "Just leave."

"Enzo?" Vigo called.

He came running.

"Let's go."

Enzo hesitated. His gaze lingered on Cressida's bloody, trembling form as she softly wept.

"We'll fetch the doctor, but that's it," Vigo said. "We won't be coming back."

"Don't bother." Cressida stood, strode past Enzo on her way to the bathroom, and shut the door with a bang.

"Where are we going?" Enzo asked. He offered a hand to Vigo, and he took it.

"We don't want to be here when Remington finds out just how much being a vampire sucks," he said as Enzo pulled him to a stand.

Enzo quirked a smile. "Was that—"

"Not intentionally. You also shouldn't be in the city surrounded by too many people until you learn to control your blood lust."

Enzo furrowed his brows. "Right. So let me ask again: where are we going?"

"Home."

Author's Note

I want to thank you for picking up this book and taking a peek inside. "Casualties of Immortality" is my debut novel, and the first book in the "Northbound by Starlight" series. This series was originally planned as a stand-alone novel where the reader follows the stories of three main characters who meet up near the end of the book to achieve a common goal. After working with my editor, Charlie Knight, we decided that the main characters and their stories not only deserved, but needed, their own books.

The stand-alone novel that was planned began as a short story I wrote for one of my college classes. That short story was titled "Rare Blood" and featured most of the main cast you will meet throughout this series. When "Rare Blood" was being worked into a novel, it was titled "Northbound by Starlight". I have since used the name for the series name. I hope you enjoyed this read, and come back future installments of the series. Wherever your next book takes you, I hope you enjoy the journey.

Please consider joining my newsletter where you'll receive first looks into future books, character art, cover reveals, and more! You can join at s-storm-crow-quill.kit.com/0870671bde

You can also find my newsletter linked on my socials under the name sstormcrowquill